FLYOVER FICTION

Series editor:

Ron Hansen

Lamb Bright Saviors

ROBERT VIVIAN

University of Nebraska Press   Lincoln & London

Publication of this volume
was assisted by The Virginia
Faulkner Fund, established in
memory of Virginia Faulkner,
editor in chief of the University
of Nebraska Press

Library of Congress
Cataloging-in-Publication Data
Vivian, Robert, 1967–
Lamb bright saviors / Robert
Vivian.
p. cm. —
(Flyover fiction)
(Tall grass trilogy)
ISBN 978-0-8032-1380-7
(pbk. : alk. paper)
1. Priests—Fiction.
2. Psychological fiction.
I. Title.
PS3572.I875L36 2010
813'.54—dc22
2009034165
Set in Minion and VAG Rounded
by Bob Reitz.

This book is for beloved T,
the girl from Big Rapids —
And for William Palmer and Carol Bender,
who have taught me more than they will ever know.

When the hearer
has become thirsty and craving,
the preacher,
even if he be as good as dead,
becomes eloquent.

RUMI

As long as we remain sheep,
we overcome.

JOHN CHRYSOSTOM

Contents

Lamb Bright Saviors

Noon Song

The preacher came up the dusty road followed by the girl pulling the wagon stacked with bibles. The preacher walked ahead of her, working it from side to side like he was addressing the last assembly on earth, staying ahead of the girl, who struggled to keep up. From far away the heat made their footsteps tremble on the dusty road like candle flames, caesura and counter-caesura in the moth-betoken fluttering of the wayfarer world. The girl stopped once or twice to catch her breath but the preacher kept striding ahead on long scissor legs toward the kingdom of God. He was shouting about salvation into the clear bright air above his head, but the words got lost in the ransack cadence of his apocalyptic cries. The bibles looked like a pyramid of gold-green bars stacked by an Egyptian slave. They were stacked neatly and covered with taut mosquito netting in the beat-up wagon, like newly minted gold.

The girl leaned into her load with the leather headband

strapped across her forehead, her arms free and swinging in the determined tug of perpetual incline all the way to the horizon. The wheels creaked and groaned when the girl made the extra push to make up lost ground, but she was still a good twenty feet behind and fading. In a few miles he'd be in another county and she'd be left behind. Then the race to nowhere would be over, and he'd be victorious over the drop-dead miles. The girl had black renegade hair all the way down her back and was around thirteen years old, though she didn't know her date of birth or town of origin. Her white summer dress was torn at the hem and she wore pink flip-flops that made the sound of cards in the spokes of a bicycle tire dealing out one bad card after another.

The preacher wore an old-time getup straight out of a traveling circus, replete with frilly mustard-colored vest, silver watch chain, and cream-colored tie, his straw hat slightly askew on his head, with dark moons of sweat under his arms. Flies gathered there to wash the TV screens of their eyes. The preacher was six-foot-seven with a wreath of white hair around his bald pate to match his albino face as the searing Nebraska heat flame-broiled Jesus inside his mouth. His coat and pants were yellow all the way down to his lemon wingtip shoes as he went banana sailing into the sun. He was preaching it up for the record books, his arms a flurry of restless birds for the sake of invisible deaf folks, like he was talking to a congregation in the dream church of his mind. His teeth flashed and snapped before the girl like a thousand shiny doors. Somehow four or five crisp bills of each denomination got loose from his waving arms and sputtered, fan-like, in the air, drifting all the way back to the girl, who did nothing to retrieve them.

No way to tell where they were going or where they had been, but it must have encompassed the world: the preacher and the girl were far out on the sea of a lonely country road where hardly a soul deigned to pass. Ditch weed and corn rows watched them go by in a gauntlet of vegetable eyes. He didn't look back at the girl to see how she was doing. His neglect was monstrous and profound, like ignoring her was central to his call.

Before long the preacher pulled up in the middle of the road, whipped out his johnson, and started pissing on the ground without ceremony while keeping up his rhapsody about all of creation. What you could hear of it was ecstatic and full of oaths, as close to babble as praise will ever get. He could have been leaning over a pulpit with crazed yellow fingernails. Turning his head from side to side he ordained both east and west to get the message out, though what the message was had never been established. Meanwhile his member dangled in front of him like scandalous bruised tackle in the plumb harvest kingdom of the uncircumcised. The girl almost caught up with him to see this baleful sight for herself before he shook off a jibber or two and put his joint back in, ready to step it up again with renewed vigor.

But he didn't get very far.

Ten feet into it he started to stagger back and forth like a drunk man and ended up doing a fey pirouette before falling face-down in the road, his hat tumbling off his head. The girl took off her headband and raced over to him, leaning down over him as her dress ballooned up with air. She put her head against his chest to listen to his heartbeat, rose up again, flipped her hair back, and settled in to listen again to his quiet rib cage of dread.

They stayed like that for a long time, a tableau of fallen travelers locked together. When she looked up her face was full of anguish, grieving for the one who had so recently been in high fever mode for the Lord. She lay back across him and covered him with her sobs, quaking with grief. Some rough-looking men fishing down by the reservoir saw what had happened and came to investigate, eventually carrying the preacher to a blind lady's house who lived about a mile away before some thunderheads rolled in and it started to pour. Though what happened after that would shake them all up forever.

Mady

When you come to a small town for the first time, far away from any other place, you have to be careful to keep the joy in till you find somewhere safe where you can let it out in secret, like maybe in a diner with an old man sitting alone and staring out the window. Every diner has one old man sitting at a booth next to the window, with what happened to him long ago buried so deep inside him it ends up in the lines of his wrinkled face.

In the old man's eyes you can see the window curving back, piling up the distance where a pretty girl sits in a room somewhere, her laughter ringing up near the ceiling then fading away in the wind outside. That's how it happens. The room is locked up or gone but he keeps trying the door because the pretty girl's in there talking to him in her pure canary-bird voice, which he loves and hates at the same time, like the voice of every pretty girl. That's what he keeps thinking about after everyone has died or left him.

The first hour after you come into town is usually the best because you don't know what will happen, though you've been in lots of towns before. Don't take the joy out and spill it over the table because you're liable to knock people down with sudden bolts of gladness. Unless you know CPR or can give mouth-to-mouth, I wouldn't risk it. Get a lay of the land and have a Coke first, or, if they have it under glass, a piece of key lime pie. Then take a careful gander around the room and size up the situation while the joy shoots off sparklers inside you.

Who's in the diner and what else do you see?

The waitress's hands look like tired ropes, along with the back of her elbows, which remind you of this chimp you once saw at a circus. She's moving between the tables with a pot of coffee in her hand. Chances are she'd give you a smoke in a pinch. She has two teenage girls at home, but one of them is about to get pregnant and she sees the baby screaming bloody murder out of his teething mouth a few weeks after he's born. Then there's this construction worker covered in dry wall wearing a baseball hat that says St. Louis Cardinals on it, who dreams about bikini girls and foreign sports cars. In fifty years he'll swap places with the old man sitting by himself and the diner will officially become immortal. The other waitress is only five or six years older than you and pretty in a cover girl kind of way: her hair's the color of tasseled corn and tied up in a ponytail. The dust-covered worker watches her behind as it tick tocks back and forth in her jeans and takes another greasy bite of his hamburger.

She's racing around the diner, refilling cups though there's only four other people in the whole place, so where's the fire? Last night she was at a party where a guy punched a hole in the wall to impress her. Someday that hole will come back to her again, growing into something else until it opens a place in her heart.

The businessman in the corner is on a different vibe altogether, more like a barren landscape where he walks alone all day with puffs of moon dust trailing behind his dress shoes. A phone rings in his ear for eight hours straight with calls from customers as office reports fall around him like leaves. He can't smell anything but paperclips and plastic, like he's breathing teargas all day. He wants to rip off all his clothes and sit naked in the diner, but that's not likely to happen. The only other people in the diner are a big woman who is alone in another booth on the other side of the room and a skinny black man at the counter. The woman has jangling bracelets on her arms that sound like hubcaps falling down a stairwell. She's had two pieces of pie and is eyeing a third. Every time she takes a bite a part of her starts crying and if you're super quiet and still you can hear the wail from where you sit. Before the pie she had the Chicken Salad Special along with a couple of Diet Cokes and some crackers. She's eating herself to death even as it's opening up craters inside her.

The skinny black man sitting at the counter has a bunch of bright-colored brooms standing up next to him. They look like another person or maybe a scarecrow except they're missing heads and arms. You can tell he tries selling them door to door, but the brooms are nothing fancy, just some strands tied together with multicolored string. He's dressed real nice, but his shoes look like he's traveled a long way, maybe as much as you have. You can't tell how old he is, somewhere between fifty or a hundred, with kinky white hair coming out from under an umpire's baseball hat. He's so thin you could shave a piece of ham with his arms. You have the feeling you could share the joy with the broom man because he looks like he might understand it, but that would still be taking a big chance and you've only been in town for twenty minutes.

Meanwhile a few flies buzz around the windows trying to get out and the ceiling fan whirs so fast it looks like it's about to take off. You can hear dishes in the kitchen and something frying on the stove, but beneath it all is this deep-down quiet that feels kinda holy and kinda sad, too. It's a nice small town as far as towns go, a good place to kick up your heels awhile and maybe live out the rest of your natural born days. The last thing you wanna do right then is get up and walk away. Mr. Gene is flexing his jaw muscles again, like he's chomping at the bit to try out his speeches. He's thinking of a new way to say Amen or Jesus, but it's not coming easily.

He doesn't pay much attention to you in the diner, but that's okay. You're just a kid hauling a bunch of bibles in a wagon you call Junior Wobbly. You have enough work to do just to keep the joy from busting out and spilling all over. There's a song you can sing to help keep the joy preoccupied, though it's better to hum it because the words could give you away—

> I'm just a girl in a new small town
> With the joy of heaven inside me
> I won't let it out till the time is right
> in a place like Katmandu or Miami.

Choirs of angels have gathered round the streets outside, but no one else can see them. They don't have fancy harps or nothin' like that, they just tend to glow in halos shaking under the eaves. Tell yourself in no-nonsense words about who you are and what's going on: *I'm Mady Kim Seymour and I carry the secret joy no one can touch swimming inside me.* The joy will take care of the rest on sawhorses in your brain. Somewhere along the way you learned good manners, but it wasn't from your mama, because Mr. Gene kidnapped you away for the Lord when you were just a snot-nosed toddler. You can still see him coming into the burning room and sweeping you up in his arms while the walls turn to forest fires in the house he had burned down just for you.

The menu is stained with ketchup at the bottom of the page over the egg breakfast that goes for $2.99. Throw in some hash browns for an extra buck and a quarter and you're in heaven. The ketchup stain has turned into glowing red on your fingertips, but it's a red you can live with.

Where does the joy come from anyway?

Nobody can say, but walking from town to town tends to shine its spinning propellers some. Who could be hungrier or more alive than you after walking eight miles in the open air while Mr. Gene tries out his speeches on the birds flying overhead? That's when you have to practice slow, careful breathing and pretend you're sitting Indian-style on the floor. Sunlight pours into the diner in coffin lids of brightness so big they chop the older waitress in half. It's a good idea to be expert at making hangdog faces so nobody will think you're having too much fun for no good reason. Think of cold rain trickling down the back of your neck with miles ahead of you then add a dead grandmother or two and you should be good to go.

The time of day you come into the town is important because you don't want to come in either too early or too late. I almost forgot to mention that. Around two is best, or maybe a little after, when people are sleepy after lunch. Park Junior Wobbly out back and strap it down with the seat belt you found outside a Memphis scrap yard. Mr. Gene said it's tailor-made for bibles and it's hard to disagree.

Cherry pie crumbs dot the sides of his mouth like a couple of nicks from shaving. Somewhere along the way he forgot how to shave his whole face so there are patches of fuzz on his cheek above his polka-dotted bow tie. It's like Mr. Gene got kicked in the head by a horse when he was young, or maybe struck by lightning: what he says and tries to say don't usually make sense unless you can understand the language of cicadas and croaking frogs and screams rolling down a mountainside.

In the meantime the joy is simmering below your sundress inside your skin and even deeper than that: it goes so far inside it's like when you peel back the layers of an onion and it makes you wanna cry. People are happy and sad around you, but that's not the same as joy: it's more like this little dog that keeps chasing its tail in circles no matter what else is going on around it. Late at night Mr. Gene'll call the new town Jerusalem in his sleep and wake up moaning. Pretend you didn't hear him. You don't want to embarrass the one you love so much.

Mr. Gene thinks he can preach in every town we go to, but the truth is most towns don't understand a word he says. Most of the time people poke fun at him or try to pretend he isn't there, and sometimes it doesn't work out so good. That's when the joy's in danger and seems to go missing for a while. You might be walking out of the same town you just walked into half an hour before, with miles to go before the next one. The joy sinks down a little so you think it's disappeared over the horizon, even though it was there just a minute ago.

Then you're like somebody living on the street with no home, no food, no money. Or like an old woman in a retirement home who no one ever comes to visit. You feel guilty for feeling the joy in the first place, like it brought you a streak of bad luck. You tell yourself you're not going to let it get the upper hand anymore, no more singing silly songs in your veins.

You think of all the towns you've been to with Mr. Gene, so many you can't keep count, how the roads leading in look all the same, with maybe a few steep hills or a cherry grove thrown in, all with the same shattered glass on the side of the road and the same small pebbles that sparkle like diamonds. And the cars passing by you are drawn-out waves that sometimes honk because you make such an odd pair walking along, a girl hauling a wagon full of bibles with a leather strap across her head for pulling power and Mr. Gene strolling ahead of you, practicing out his preaching, making gestures with his arms or walking with them pinned behind his back, like he's captain of a ship somewhere out at sea.

Then before you know it you feel the joy creeping up again with all these ferns shining off in the woods, like every part of them is clapping without a sound. So you end up saying to it, Okay, joy, go and do your thing, I can't keep you out anymore: Hartwick Pines 4 Miles, Broken Bow 10 miles, Walnut Grove 3 miles. Because there's really only one small town and you're always walking into it for the first time, the town that will make you or break you or welcome you with 4th of July flags waving on every front porch. That's just how the joy works, playing hide-n-seek because it's so damned shy, but it knows how to do a number on you and all your best intentions, which end up like so much dust blowing in the wind.

So when you see Mr. Gene rolling his head back and forth on the blind lady's bed after some rough customers carried him in and he tries to get the words out in a pouring flood, you try to remember all the joyful times you had with him walking into towns. You don't care what he's trying to say because he's still alive. You sit at the foot of the bed and wait for him to make sense because you know how long he's been waiting and rehearsing for this very moment.

Then guess what?

The joy you thought was so dangerous is the same thing he's trying to tell them about, the one that keeps showing up all over the place no matter what's going on, in leaves and weather and somebody picking their nose when they think nobody's looking. Then you know nothing can touch the joy and nothing can hurt it, not even dying, which is what you gotta keep telling yourself the night Mr. Gene lays there on his deathbed, opening his mouth so feverish and wide it's like all he wants to do is sing.

Oly

The preacher was like a bucket full of worms sloshing back and forth on the blind lady's bed, sheets wet with fever, and his skinny candle legs crisscrossed and sawing, with the rain coming down hard against the roof, the four of us standing there like the night we broke into her house long ago. I had a hard time trying not to laugh because what he was saying was funny, the words coming out of his mouth like sparks from a welder's mask.

He said he had picked us out of a lineup in the sky to die in front of, plucking us out of the clean lofty air for the blind lady's house, where we had once staged the end of the world. I didn't know you could pick the people you were gonna die in front of like caramel at the candy store and that's funny too, damn near hilarious, so funny I don't know where to put the laughter pumping up the blood vessels of my head in mass hysteria, because he was funny and there was just no denying it.

When I die I want to be watching a Huskers' game in a bar, doesn't matter which one as long as it's tuned in to Big Red, dying right in the middle of a scoring drive marching down for six in a cloud of glory and the point after, with all those red balloons floating up out of Memorial Stadium in another sea of waving red in the delirious dreams of thousands. Then you could get rid of my body however you wanted, just so I'd die knowing they were gonna score.

But preacher-side I had a hard time trying not to laugh, coming so close a few times it sounded like I was choking back sobs. You just had to see him laying there listening to what he had to say and how it came out of his mouth in droves of swooping barn swallows. I had tears burning up in my eyes in my own personal gas mask fit for race riots and snarling dogs in old-time grainy newsreels. I said to myself, Whatever you do don't laugh, Oly, it's stone-cold serious in here, think of the crimes we committed in this lonely house with comfy throw rugs all around. But you can't believe how hard it was, walking the tightrope of my comical self and watch it now, careful because it's death we're talking about here and death ain't funny, fool, I tell you that all the time.

The blind lady sat in her chair, glowing like a cloud off yonder on the verge of becoming rain. But I have to admit it, hell yes, even that was funny, just no denying it no matter how you carve it up into paving stones: funny to be back at the blind lady's house, funny to watch the preacher reach up with his trembling hand pointing to the throne of heaven past the wintry branch of thy withered finger, he called it, funny that the blind lady couldn't see us but was still watching us with every pore of her old lady's skin—funny, so funny, shit, I coulda pissed my pants just standing there, pretending like I'm coughing but trying to ease the ya-yas out one at a time before they go supernova on me, Munoz looking at me squint-eyed like a pissed-off Chinaman, so goddamned funny, but Danny had his eyes glued on the blind woman—I think he wants to read by fingertip just like she does—and Yarborough with his own fingers hooked inside his belt wrangler-style, like, Easy does it, man, easy does it: I been in this situation before, so just hold on—and the whole thing funnier still when you saw it all from a certain point of view, like a spirit floating up around the ceiling with the girl sitting at the end of the bed like a piece of sailboat, the wind still in its sails, rocking in the water.

We'd been down fishing at the tank where we used to go a long time ago, catching nothing but sunburn, when we heard the preacher cry out up on the road about a football field or a Hail Mary pass away. He'd passed out in his electric banana suit, or whatever you want to call it, and the girl was leaning over to help him. We looked back and you could see them shining in the sun there on the road with bits of cattail spores floating in the air like stardust memories. The preacher's hat had fallen off beside him, the mouth of it in the dirt like it was waiting for somebody to pass by and toss in some spare change. We hadn't caught a doggone thing anyway, plus we were hung over big time from the night before. That's when I knew it was gonna be potentially funny or fatal, Yarborough coming down hard on me later as we were about to carry

His Lord Spaceship into the blind woman's house, hissing *What's so funny, asshole* and I couldn't tell him just then, just tried to shrug it off as the rain started to pour down.

Gus was the first to reach them on the road and I felt the laughter bubbling up inside me even then, a little rumble or quake with overtones of seismic tremors in it, though there should have been nothing funny about a stranger passed out on the road in a suit that looked like it was made out of technicolored ice cream. In my mind I tried to apologize to the fallen man beforehand, that the coming onslaught of my guffaws was nothing against him, even before we discovered that he had a bible inside his mouth and was some kind of latter-day prophet, which should have sobered me up but instead just added another layer of humor to the situation, like sticking rags in a gas can before you strike a match.

I did my Christian best not to look at the girl's ass bending over like that, but I figured one clean sweep of her budding harvest wouldn't hurt nobody, especially if my eyes didn't linger there, which of course they did, like a hound dog on the scent of a bleeding coon. In this part of the country you get your fair share of preachers passing in and out of town on their way to other troubled ears, so he didn't register as anything special, except for the girl and the color of his outfit, like he was a champagne king rising to the top of a cunt-shaped glass.

At the dugout I have this paper sack I call Rosie that I breathe into so I don't hyperventilate, and that's part of the laughter I've been fighting on and off for years, the humor I can't get rid of that's always threatening to turn me into a

17

sobbing lunatic. This paper sack is like a wrinkled-up asshole but it gives me space and time to breathe and you can't buy that with a lung machine or even fancy diving equipment, all that scuba gear with air compressors hammering oxygen down into the deep blue sea. I wish I'd had it with me at the blind lady's house but I was afraid to ask her for a paper sack for fear of raising everyone's suspicions or Yarborough's righteous wrath.

But they're like brothers to me—I'd do anything for each one of them and have, time and time again. I don't have no other family to lay a claim to. Those boys is all I got. Gus visits me at the dugout but he don't stay long anymore, even when I ask him to hang around so we can break down some more game film. I guess my living conditions depress the shit out of him because he's fidgety there, sitting on the end of the bench with the husks of peanut shells all around him like tiny shards from a nuclear fallout, Gus looking like he's about to get a rabies shot or something like that. Once he turned his head and looked at me real slow and said in a quiet voice, *You're one fucked-up pilgrim, Oly,* but I don't think he meant anything by it, not really anyway.

I used to be happy living in a trailer with a good-looking woman and sometimes I was even sober for more than twenty-four hours, but I was let go from my job at the grain elevator and lost my looks and almost my mind from doing too many drugs and anything else I could get a hand on that could give a boost to my chemical well-being. A dealer from Denver told me I looked like the trumpet player Chet Baker just before he died, but who the hell is Chet Baker anyway and why haven't I heard of him? Don't trumpet me no strumpet, is what I told him, don't cornhole me in this endless field of corn. I still don't know if he was paying me a compliment or reaming my sorry ass.

But for someone who was dying the preacher sure was a talkative sonofabitch, I will say that. He just went on and on, trailing dribble and flashbacks out of his mouth, of other beds where he laid, practicing to die. He said so out of his own Christ-spittled lips. It's hard not laughing when you want to, about the hardest thing a body can keep from doing when it comes at you with the jim-jams and body quakes and the hoochie koochie man thrown in. It's not often you get to hear someone go on like that, especially when he's dying. So beyond the humor and hilarity of the situation I had to admit it was a privilege and something you don't see every day, unless you're a guardian angel or some other kind of invisible wallpaper.

I kept thinking of the pussy posse back at the dugout, stacked up by my army cot, but there was no way I could go to them. And for the first time in forever I didn't even want to. I couldn't pass up an opportunity like watching the preacher die, spewing his river stream of prayers and blessings I never heard of before. I half expected him to break up into rainbows of streaking oil stains like the kind you see at Jiffy Lube, but that didn't happen.

So I made firm and told myself the pussy posse would have to wait, the spunked-on pages of their defilement pulling at me like the pouting faces of garden nymphs. I started to think of them in a different way then, in the blind lady's house with the preacher dying and the rain coming down, with the girl at the end of the bed locked in for the deathwatch. I'd always been on the lookout for pictures of naked women in the throes of twisted passion on demented principle alone to fulfill my every need, but I have to admit it hasn't happened yet and probably never will.

As the preacher was giving last witness to his final hours I pictured two of them rising out of his mouth like genies from a bottle, going down on each other with me as giant moon man watching them float into the air above his life-draining face as it testified to the air, two naked girls who were so lost doing things to each other with strange naked men lurking in the background that it wasn't even a question of getting off anymore but something else spiraling out of control, something you see stamped in the dot matrix eyes of missing children down at the post office. On the other side of fucking is a little mewing sound you can barely make out, like an abandoned kitten in the middle of the night that's not gonna make it, this feeble, precious sound coming out of its perfect button mouth, past the furl of a milk-lapping tongue.

Some door opened up inside me watching the preacher die that had never been so much as knocked on. I heard the tapping from the afterlife and it sounded like a polished stone knocking against a thunderous bowl. I was almost pure and shiny again, listening to him go on the way he did without a lustful thought to my name though the humor was still alive and kicking. I needed to goddamn laugh before I started bawling, like those electric paddles they zap you with to get

20

your heart pumping again. The laughter was changing in my gullet and light-years away from mockery or dancing naked with a lampshade on your head.

I didn't want the pussy posse to crucify me in the waste of my spilled seed, which I knew had grown nations of little towheaded Olys in the weeds, laughing their pink asses off in fields of hysterical corn. I wanted to speak to them in three dimensions where they could tell me what they wanted beyond the ecstasy of their pronghorn fuck faces with scrunched up eyebrows penciled down in flesh-hammering vs.

I became sorrowful in front of my best friends and the preacher laid out like some hopped-up version of a yapping bed, the girl and her bullet-bright skin, the blind lady shining in the corner like she'd become a life-sized candle without no wick to taper off from. I wasn't born like this, I'd tell them. Something happened along the way. Let a patch of sunlight bore a hole of blinding truth through my forehead, I'll bow down before this divine brain surgery and welcome the searing pain. I swear it on the discoloration of my right big toe, which you're welcome to chop off or run over with a snowmobile.

I'm dearly sorry about my jim-jam, the sea-salt detergent that washes through the dens of the damned. I thought you understood that's what happens in 7-11s all over the country. I didn't used to be this way. I give you my moth-eaten word. But where does that leave us? I don't goddamn know. We're here to watch a strange man die, to give proof to a truth I never lived till now.

I looked at my brothers, each one of us lost and tattooed

past recognition, Gus's whole body practically covered in comic book explosions, and I said to myself, *They're as lost and weeping as I am, they're as worn down at the core.* I saw their faces in profile, almost like they was lined up to face a firing squad, though the rifles were made of female staying power and stillness in the blind lady and the little girl at the foot of the bed.

Why couldn't we have been different somehow, leave well enough the fuck alone, including the blind woman and her towering spirit that dwarfs these seafaring plains? I tried so hard to be like you, but we only brought out the worst in each other until the night Gus held me in his arms while I laughed and cried in the dugout and he kissed my tired forehead.

So stand up straight and do not laugh. Don't look at Munoz anymore for the faint Mexican mustache he's created out of pubic hair.

Yarborough looks like one of the Allman Brothers, waylaying his guitar.

Danny, Gus, don't fall for the blind lady so hard, she's not liable to see where your relationship is headed.

And little girl, how long must you have waited to see the preacher like that, laid out between his feet that look like perch curving at the end of the line? Run, get out of this house, or go over to the blind woman who's turning into some kind of saving cloud. She's just sitting there in her glowing shawl where we once tried to hurt her. Somehow we grew up wrong, war, prison, and dugouts, with Irving Friar pulling one in at the fifty-yard line to take it all the way.

She's as good a woman as there ever was. Let the preacher roar in his tattered death robes, his mouth can't touch us though the singing words can.

Go to Ms. Marian, go to the blind woman. Seek refuge in her eyes, flashing like the mane of a purple horse. She'll feel your presence. Then kneel down next to her, let her lay a wrinkled hand on your head and hold it there for as long as it takes while the preacher goes on dying and we, the others, every last one, look on like clueless fools who tried to fuck up Paradise only to find out there's no way we ever the fuck could.

Godsick

I lay in the blind woman's bed and my dying filled the room like singing glass. Their faces were the color of blank, except for the blind woman, who sat drinking my dying in cracked lips that had whispered God every day of her life. Memories flitted by in the gloaming inside those faces, haunt of footfalls and laughter from other rooms, long drives down country roads where clouds of dust came up righteous. Their heads shifted like corn piping in the wind. I could see through them all the way to ignorance. Clean laundry on the line, Mama humming with a pin in her mouth, the song a gospel tune late to come by off the a.m. dial: picture of loveliness that never ends.

Jesus sat beggared in the corner, the holes in his hands the circumference of dimes for the wounds of every living thing to enter and disappear. He was wearing tattered jeans and black dusty flip-flops. He had just come in off the highway, hitchhiking all the way from Gethsemane. His beloved thighs shone through the worn fabric of those jeans. His blood seeped out across the floor of the world as clarity came off him in beads of percolating rain.

> I am the lamb of the highway,
> I told them, but they did not understand.
> They did not know that all of us would become
> one in the divine and fatal accident.

For many hours I tried to tell them but I did not speak in words: no, only light that came and went and came again, auguries of hope in every pane of glass. Mercy betrothed me like a groom. I remembered a pair of headlights cresting the slope of a hill somewhere in Alabama, blooming on the horizon like the silent approach of death. Who came for me but the light that never ends? The walls stood listening on pillars of dust as curtains danced like cool piano keys shimmering out glissandos. They were women once in the steadfast diadems of candle flames.

The bed smelled of gabardine and old lace. Jesus' fingers were tapered like the wings of a starving dove that refused to fly. It wasn't just a lance in his side but a broken belt buckle shaped in the form of a missile's fin. Dunes of prairie wind moaned against the house on their way to other sands, spray of translucent pebbles tapping at the window. Inside one of them the wind will know its final resting place, stunning into stillness. I thought I heard the sough of traffic, but it was just the wind rifling around in eddies made of moans. I always heard traffic as cosmic soundtrack, hot dry waves rolling out to rush hour and mortality. Hearing traffic was sometimes all I had, knowing which model and make was coming up behind us, even cattle trucks carrying livestock ready to be cut up into steaks and hamburger. Someone had died in the blind lady's bed long before me but I didn't know who it was. I felt it in the bolts of sheets that had once held the expiring body, the blind woman an expert of deathbeds and savant of other men's deaths, her husband or grown son perhaps, someone whose body she knew once inside her own. The fact that she never drove a car filled me with a tingling sensation. I felt her marrowing sorrow in the fillings of my teeth.

I preached the gospel of the highway and, walking away, felt like Paul struck down on the road to Damascus—the destiny of every driver. I told them Damascus ran all along I-80 out to Denver and beyond. I looked to see if Jesus was digging it but his beautiful eyes were miles away. I preached speed limits and exit signs, state troopers hiding behind billboards in bullet-shaped sedans with clean-shaven chins like the split asses of baby antelope, construction pylons, and semis transporting frozen peas to augment a poor region's fast food diet, blinking hazard lights and weigh stations, bumper stickers spelling out the hyperbole of talking frogs, road rage rolling into ditches where each driver suffers a crushed lung fanning out in farting playing cards. Click it or ticket, air bags exploding in life rafts that leave powder burns at the temples à la Frankenstein. Recall is another word for repentance. F.O.R.D. is an acronym for

For Our Radical Deliverance

but you will not see it written in any owner's manual.

Those who drive the highways are traveling to God without knowing it, hands clasped around steering wheels turning under star charts of smashed windshields, near-death experiences, the being of light with hands made of dust motes.

Was it worth it?

He asks, she asks: your life is the answer in continuous snapshots behind closed doors and running with your shirt off. Beware of cigarette taxes between borders, of greasy spoons with runny eggs, waitresses who look like tired Madonnas in the contemplation of their men gone awry, plotting serial killers staking out new hunting grounds, underpasses and the illicit hands of strangers spidering down below your waist in a tell-tale comeuppance when you're bone lonely next to graffiti, litter scrawling the story of the world, and roadkill divine that will one day become stampeding herds again, trampling everyone in sight.

Jesus is a hitchhiker on the side of the road. He wants to drive away with you. He'll pick up what's left of you in a nail-biter's Chevy. He looks all over America to resurrect a nation of killed drivers. You can hear the rusty tailgates bang out the clashing of cymbals, highway crosses flung like jacks across the countryside in the glory of reckless abandon. People are lost every day on the highway, their names alluded to by talking heads on the radio who aren't tuned in to the magnitude of this reality. They disappear at rest areas, show up dead five hundred miles away in refrigerated trucks. They leave their cars on the shoulders and walk away, never to be seen again.

I lost my license in Louisiana for drunk driving and then I could live the life I was meant for: I was saved. I've walked our nation's highways with Mady Kim ever since. She has grown up around the mystical air waves of power lines humming beside us, other crosses waiting for little-known tribes to be crucified.

Mirages above heated tar bequeathed us the courage to keep on. The face of Jesus can be discerned in oil stains, cumulus clouds, mangled wrecks in the seeing-eye of gaping metal torn from a chassis. I go ancient into dashboards where the talk show hosts shout out prophecies between static and commercials. You will not lose your hair, your money, your patent on said whirligig: all these shall be restored to you when you die in a head-on collision.

Baaa, I cried.

I did not choose the highway, the highway chose me.

But they did not understand. How could they? Jesus was ringing the dinner bell. He lifted it in his pouring dark hand to hear his eternal echo in the tolling of a bell. To end on this outpost of grass, dirt of earth peeled back to sky. State Farm doesn't cover divine sightings, but Jesus is there in the corner of every policy, hiding in plain sight. My skin was stretched taut over the ineffable clabbered city of void, besieged by crows picking at my intestines in the middle of the road.

I loved the boys I came to die in front of. How could I not? My skin trailed the tracer heat of every star. Mama would not let the blackbirds near the house for fear that they would bring us bad luck. We learned to count them off like ticking hands on a clock. They knew time in sundials of looping branches. We grew up under auspices of wings.

You are not your body.

You are not even yourself, I tried to say. I tried to tell them. Get thee to a rest stop. Objects in mirror are closer than they appear. I babbled in the history of pavement and mile markers.

I saw myself in glimpses, shards of man upon the blind woman's bed in liver spots of fading skin. I wanted to tell them about my sins so they could try them on and throw them away forever.

> Lamb bright saviors, what has become of you?
> Are you going to die on the highway like the
>   rest of them?
> Why do you go shepherdless into the mouth
>   of the din when God's Son is there
>   in the corner?
> Did you not know that the beast is upon
>   you—with ragged breath smelling
>   of ethanol containers?

I did not come to console you with lies but to lay waste to falsehood. Cities will burn in the distance. The smoke of holocausts. A nation of crosses bent and blinding in the sun past rows of defunct windmills where Satan's grin is broadest. Gutted factories smoking under an orange sky. Rife litter in the aftermath blowing to the ends of the earth. Only highway crosses to show the way, a new country rising out of the ashes.

The blind woman understood but she was not saying. Mady pulling the wagon of bibles, her bare feet at night like Christ's body laid out in a clean white shroud. Young men with violence in their faces standing next to me with distrust in their eyes, misunderstanding, the emptiness of cell phones and drug addiction, haste in everything they do.

New lambs to the slaughter. But they will lead you. *Enemy, thy name is suburb.* Move to hinterlands in order to be saved. Nebraska is shaped like an arrowhead, chipped before the first white man was here. The bleeding heart of the heartland. Countenances of misbelievers, drug-ridden young men with hard times ahead of them, violence in this room a long time ago, its echo like the dull report of hammering nails. The word is accomplished and you are wing-light in the rush that makes this body shine. Dying on the blind woman's bed was the greatest thing that ever happened to me, glowing bits of light rising up through the gaping pores of my skin.

Yarborough

If people are gonna watch you die then you'd better make it good. I think that's a reasonable thing to expect for one of those who hauled your ass into the old blind lady's house so you could do your shouting and dying on someone else's bed.

That's how I see it anyway, with the preacher we found on the road and the girl trailing behind with that wagonload of bibles. Second I saw 'em I thought, *What a sorry act of shit to be dragging all that cargo out near the tail end of nowhere.* I wasn't thinking of justice then, the righteous and bona fide kind that doesn't take place in any court of law but shows up when you least expect it in a blind lady's house to take you back to the scene of the crime that was your own brainchild from the beginning.

That's the hard shaft-end truth of it. Before that, Gus and Oly were away from me and Munoz, maybe three hundred yards out on the reservoir. We were fishing for spoonbill like we used to, first time in something like twenty years. You almost could've called it a fucked-up kind of reunion, what with Munoz back from the war, me just out of prison, Gus living with his aunt, and Oly bouncing from job to job and woman to woman. Not a one of us had a direction you'd call promising, like we were all going down the drain at the same time in our own special way. But I never expected nothing anyway: I knew I'd be back in the clink before the year was out.

Night before we got drunk 'till four in the morning, trying to get war stories out of Munoz, but he was so far gone you were better off watching CNN. Taking care of those IEDs must have fucked up his head big-time. Maybe he was there when they decapitated that marine, I don't know. One thing's for sure: we weren't in no kind of shape to stand on a concrete retaining wall all day in ninety-degree heat, hung over and getting fried up in the sun.

We were about to pack it in before we heard Mr. Thou Art back up behind us on the road with that flip-flopping girl trailing behind. Least I was. Here we spent all day fishing, not saying a word, and we end up catching a dying preacher instead, babbling out a stream of nonsense right there on the road. I couldn't make out what he was saying, except maybe a word here and there. But I wasn't really listening. I was thinking of the blind lady as we carried the preacher up the stairs, wondering what she'd make of us after all these years with yours truly as the ringleader, standing there and waiting for the preacher to die while she sat in the same

Yarborough

goddamn chair she sat in the night we broke in, like nothing
had changed but the date on the calendar. She knew it was
my idea from the get-go, and the knowledge grew between
us to take on a life of its own that I still can't put into words,
but call it a curse, call it a boomerang effect, call it whatever
the hell you want that includes the beginning of the end and
the end dragged out like doing hard time.

I didn't set out to touch her.

That was never part of my plan for all my swaggering talk.
I never could get anybody to understand that. I was just as
surprised as she was when I went for her. It doesn't make
sense even now. The opportunity just presented itself in a
purple haze of possibility and I broke through that fog when
I touched her throat.

So I wasn't really paying attention to the preacher as he
laid there dying, shooting his holy roller mouth off. He was
just a jabbering monkey between me and Ms. Marian, his
voice rising and falling like a cheap music box cranked up
too tight, piping out a broken song that had something to
do with Jesus. When we brought him in a part of me knew
this was the grim reaper variety of justice I'd been waiting
for all those years, standing there in her tiny frame house
for the first time since that night with the stained wooden
beams so low you could hang a man with a good six inches
for dangling.

I could feel the blind lady's eyes all over me. Her eyes are like
lemons in a fruit machine coming up all dollar signs, or the
cast-off skin of some diamondback withering in the sun. They
don't have to see like other eyes—they have visions all their

33

own. We'll always be connected no matter what and there's nothing nobody can ever do about it, not even God.

I thought about her every night while I was doing time, replaying what happened in that room. I never told nobody what happened between us: it was between me and her and I wanted it to stay that way. Out in the yard throwing iron I got to thinking that nothin' in the world ever touched me but the sight of her walking toward me and what we did that night—and what we didn't do, too. I could see her clear as day, wrapped up in that lacy white shawl like the Mother of God herself, her eyes doing a queer number on me as the rest of them went about taking her place apart. Then her feet wrapped up in those moccasins she made with her own tiny hands—with a long white feather stuck in her hair that I later took off and put in my mouth while I was on top of her.

To make for some kind of dream catcher?

To stitch into a wing so she could fly away?

I was damned before I ever step foot in her house. Some people are born to be damned and there's not a goddamned thing you can do about it. I always figured a good man was just a rumor anyway, something from the twinkling Land of Oz.

They tell you in prison or church there's a way you can be saved or rehabilitated, but what they don't know is that not everyone can even be reached, let alone saved. Even as a kid I was already a bad man. I knew it all along. I was just waiting for it to take shape inside me. And here I was ten feet away from the first serious crime I ever committed, the kind of crime no court of law will ever argue because the victim of said crime never turned you in—never even accused you, which just keeps widening out into deeper parts of free-falling space.

I didn't give a fuck how old she was or the fact that she was blind, she was good-looking to me. I figured anybody who moved to Point Blank got what was coming to them. I told you already, it's not supposed to make sense. I left Gus standing there like a deer in the headlights, and he just stood there the whole time like he couldn't believe what was happening.

I couldn't either, for that matter. He didn't break or touch a thing, and the funny thing is, he feels the worst about it to this day. Oly and Munoz in the kitchen, going through the cabinets and throwing shit on the floor like a couple of drunk Indians. I see it all happening again before me in high def on a wide plasma screen: how we cased her place for an hour, sitting there in the dark, taking tugs from a bottle of Beam about an acre away, listening to "Mississippi Queen." So it's not like we snuck up on her, though that was the original plan. Then Oly gets out of the car, walks up a couple hundred feet, and throws a bottle of Everclear at her mailbox. And we follow after him, then just walk into her house. She'd been waiting for us all our lives, sitting there just like she is now, beyond the preacher, wrapped up in a shawl.

Maybe she was lonely. No court in the world could ever rule that out. When I got her to the back of that spare room and pushed her down onto the bed, I got on top of her and looked at her a long time, breathing hard. I can still see her pinned under me, not able to move, the way she looked up at me with those eyes that couldn't see. I could hear Oly and Munoz in the kitchen, and Gus trying to tell them to be quiet because she could recognize our voices, but by then it was way too late and they were too far gone and didn't give a shit. Neither did I. After what I already done? After what I was? We stayed there like that for a long time, my hand at her throat and her just staring up at me, not seeing anything but understanding somehow, and me, with that goddamned feather between my teeth, hearing the mayhem going on in the other room like the soundtrack to madness itself.

And I.

What the fuck you want me to say?

Taking a little old blind lady that never hurt nobody, in her own house. That couldn't even *see*. Taking all your clothes off and rubbing up against her.

But I.

The way she was under me, see. The way she was waiting for the axe to fall, for the worst thing to happen. But I. See. It's like this. You go your whole life not knowing why you do certain things, why you're made up a certain way, why you keep falling down a well that's got no water in it, only darkness and more darkness falling down all around you.

I let go of her throat and laid down next to her. I curled up in a ball, my back to her. I didn't touch her beyond that. We laid there together side by side, neither one of us moving or saying a word. But I could hear her breathing. I could, and it was a light and quiet sound, like she was afraid to make any noise but still had to breathe somehow. A kind of light, high-up breathing. It was my idea in the first place. I was the one who was gonna take her back to the room and do something to her—I was the one who nobody could ever outdo for craziness, me, Nate Yarborough, inmate number 816-555-E4. So there, I fucking said it—admitted what happened and what didn't and how it led back to her house with the preacher dying there in front of us.

We were out to fuck up what we could for no other reason than we somehow got it into our heads and she laid there right next to me breathing, like some kind of small animal that wouldn't hurt a fly. I'm the same motherfucker I've always been, breaking people's jaws in bars, busting parole. Nothing's changed in me. But the way she laid right next to me, see. The way she didn't plead or beg or even cry. I just can't get it out of my head for some reason. Sometimes it seems like us two laying there, listening to what was going on in the other rooms, was the strangest, realest thing that ever happened to me. And I don't know why. I don't.

I didn't bring her to the bed for forgiveness. But maybe that's why it's always there, just below the surface, in everything I do and see, shanks under the bunks, other guys' bitches wearing hairnets. I fought it the best I could, high and low and every place in between. The blind lady wins. She's the champion of the free world. I can't say it didn't happen the way it did because it sure the fuck almost did.

The preacher could have his deathbed all he wanted, I just couldn't pay attention. I was watching her, waiting for something to happen in the house we busted into when we were trying out our mean streak, that we 'bout nearly took apart board by board for no other reason than because we knew she lived alone. How's that for motive? I wanted to know once and for all why she didn't move or say anything, why we laid there like we'd been married since forever, or like I was some painted snake out of the bible that should have struck and killed her dead with one bite but somehow marked her hand on his cold-blooded skin, weeping venom tears for the rest of his natural born days.

Mady

Mr. Gene and me used to practice for his deathbed maybe twice a month when we were out on the road. He said it was important to get the timing down and get in touch with the cosmic pull that makes all deaths one. I think we became pretty damn good at it, balancing life and death on a shoestring and drawing it tight over the abyss, as Mr. Gene liked to say.

Dying in bed is an art form and Mr. Gene would tell you that himself if he wasn't so sick. He'd sit up for the first ten minutes and then slowly sink down as death took possession of him, laying him out good and proper so it could hop the train of his expiring spirit. Before we got started he'd try to psyche himself up by saying *Pallor of a corpse* a few dozen times while I went outside and got a bucket of ice to prepare for the meltdown. Sometimes I'd sneak away downstairs and have me a Coke and a smoke, which I never told Mr. Gene about.

I liked to be by myself sometimes, sitting on the metal staircase and watching the sun go down, thinking about other things besides death and dying and what comes in the wake of cranking up for it. I was hopping glad to be alive and thankful that we always had the road ahead of us, wherever it was going. I never could bring myself to say to Mr. Gene, *But you're not dying*, out of some kind of loyalty. Maybe I was just too embarrassed to break his string of ongoing defeats, which he was so proud of it was almost like a victory march straight from his motel bed.

Molasses, there was always molasses thick as turpentine, he wanted me to pour into his coffee after he was done, to revive his corporeal corruption, he used to say. I never understood that but I went with it anyway. Practicing for his deathbed meant so much to him, like he was practicing for more than death, practicing for a life about to go up in flames before he could get all the kinks out. He'd lay there under the bedsheet no matter how hot or how cold it was outside, trying out his death throes and rattles and letting the visions come on.

My job was to be his primary audience that grieves in disbelief, throwing in a few cries of mercy to ring up near the ceiling. I had all the deathbed moves down cold, each gesture and expression geared to the task of a life force oozing from the body of a loved one. I wiped his forehead with a towel and otherwise made sure he was comfortable during his revved-up final hour. I sat next to the bed and sometimes kneeled down and watched the plunging action of his Adam's apple like a boat cutting through rough water. Mr. Gene said

I had a good streak of patience and the ability to look death straight in the eye, but I don't know about that.

To be honest, death wasn't usually even on my mind, not even when he shuddered deep inside his throat and practiced his last few dying gasps. Then what? The sound of water dripping from the faucet in the bathroom, somebody passing by outside in the hallway, even a breaking bottle in the parking lot and the cuss words that followed from the one who dropped or threw it.

I'd think about my mama, though her face was always hazy to me, somewhere between this beautiful young woman and this model I saw once on TV. My daddy's face was even fuzzier because I'd never seen him: sometimes his face was thin and pointy like a goat with a small beard at the end of it and other times it was full of smiles and big as a pumpkin. Sometimes my daddy was even black, and that was the strangest face of all, looking down at me with a smile that was one part sugar and one part ancient. So practicing for Mr. Gene's deathbed was never any big deal once you got the drift of it. I've only told a few folks about how we practiced, and I could tell by the way they looked at me that 1) they didn't want to believe me, or 2) it just scared them and made them squeamish so they tried to change the subject.

I knew the real thing would be different when it came. But we practiced anyway. Mr. Gene needed me for his deathbed because he said the atmosphere in the room was different when I was with him, watching his every move and listening to his voice. So who was I to argue? I didn't like the idea of him practicing all by himself. Then something might really

happen and he'd start dying for real with nobody around
to help him. One time I spent almost an hour out in a field
looking for a cricket so I could bring it back in a matchbox.
And you know how that is: the last thing a cricket wants is
to be found out of its hiding place.

Mr. Gene claimed it was important to get used to flies
buzzing around because that was part of the deal: you can't
die in bed without a fly buzzing up around the ceiling somewhere. I had to make sure the bedsheet was pulled up to
his neck, that his bare feet stuck out at the end of the bed
to emphasize his mortality. He had two big toenails that
sometimes went an awful shade of blue from walking in his
fancy shoes that didn't stay fancy for long. How I moaned
was up to me, but it had to come from a deep-down place
where no songbirds ever went. And no gnashing of the teeth
either, or over-the-top hysterics: he'd provide the fireworks
and the speaking in tongues when the time was right. He
made sure his head was way back so you could see the twin
barrels of his nostrils and watch the dark hairs breathing
mystery and the snot that knew about rivers and dams and
the mating of animals.

That's how Mr. Gene explained it anyhow.

One time we were practicing in this place called the Fawn
Motel in Iowa and you could feel this sudden change in the
atmosphere. I think the temperature dropped about twenty
degrees in a little over ten minutes. Mr. Gene was at the part
in his deathbed delivery when it was like waves of holiness
rolling right off him, lapping at the shore of his eternal soul,
when suddenly this tornado siren began to sound. Before

long people started walking in groups down the hallway—the manager even knocked on our door and shouted, *Tornado! Everybody in the basement!* but neither one of us said a word. We just sat there frozen in our deathbed positions like mannequins nailed to a wailing wall.

I was waiting for Mr. Gene to snap out of it and say something, but by then it was way too late. The manager had already left, figuring nobody was inside. We had to be the last people left on the third floor, as everybody else in the Fawn Motel had hightailed it to the basement. But Mr. Gene didn't pay any mind to the siren or the manager's warning: he was too busy getting ready for the final speech that would punch out the lights from the Rock of Ages. I went to the window and that's when Mr. Gene started talking his blue streak. Sure enough I could see the tornado about eight miles away with stuff circling all around, the twister churning and blazing a trail a whole city block wide.

I got real scared then, but I'd never broken the spell of a deathbed practice before. I had this superstition that if we broke it off in the middle it might cause Mr. Gene to have a heart attack right then and there. And you know how people say a tornado sounds like a freight train coming at you? Well, it does—and then some. But it didn't affect Mr. Gene any, except to make his face go a little green as the lettuce light outside kept on getting brighter. But Mr. Gene was dedicated to his calling and there was no wiggle room even for tornadoes. I tried to tell him, I tried to say something about it, but he wouldn't listen to me. He was already locked into deathbed mode and kicking it into overdrive.

Whatever track that twister was on Mr. Gene was on his own, fixing to learn how to die better, and so the two of them were coming to a head. I couldn't leave him alone. Pretty soon the roar of the tornado and all those swirling things made Mr. Gene's voice sound like a pipsqueak's and then I couldn't hear him at all. By then it was too late to go anywhere because the tornado was coming straight for us. I did the worst thing you could do during a tornado: I stayed at the window and watched it.

I started talking to it in the calmest voice I could muster, like I knew the tornado personally. I told the twister it could go around us if it wanted, that it had plenty of room to navigate and we weren't but two little rag dolls flapping in the breeze. I told it about the deathbed even though Mr. Gene wasn't dying, that maybe it was true we weren't real smart sometimes when it came to common sense but that our hearts were in the right place.

By this time the rain was pouring at me sideways through the open window along with a few junkyards of missiles from everywhere around and far-off places besides, whirligigs of all makes and sizes, flying at me at a couple hundred mph.

The tornado looked like the face of Jesus when he set to driving out the shopkeepers from the temple—or a crazy-haired Moses parting the Red Sea, all the old-timey prophets showing up in a twister the changing color of dirt, moss, and mayhem with a few thousand swirling feet from a giant woman's shrieking hair. I called that twister a sweet son of a bitch, though I didn't really hold nothing against it but flat-out awe. Later I looked at the wall behind me and it was covered floor to ceiling with everything you could imagine, like things from a knife-throwing contest: a hundred and one tornado-made tacks, a birthday candle, somebody's cell phone, a kid's baby picture, branches from a tree, a few playing cards, and a license plate or two. They were all there, whistling by one after the other, but how they missed me standing there in the window I'll never know. Maybe I turned into bright ghostly air made of light and the missiles passed through me on their way to other bull's-eyes. But when I looked at my body and my hands I was somehow okay, no puncture wounds in me anywhere, not even a scratch.

I looked back at Mr. Gene and he was a different story, though he wasn't hurt either: he was still trying to practice his deathbed but his whole body was buried in a dune of white sand except for his head and feet, which moved like they weren't even attached to the rest of him. If you didn't know better you'd swear he'd just come from the Sahara Desert buried in all that sand, soon to be totally covered except for his lips mumbling faint words I couldn't make out. The tornado was gone by then, sucked back up into the sky as the sun started to come out, like there never had been any storm. I poked my head out the window and could see that our motel was practically the only building left standing on the whole block. Somehow the tornado had missed us—and had also whipped up this pile of sand to bury Mr. Gene. I went up to the bed and kneeled down in the dune beside him, but it was hard to get a good footing.

You okay, Mr. Gene? I asked, and when he looked at me it was like he had never seen me before. I think he didn't know what to do or say after the tornado and his deathbed practicing. Everybody knows that dying in bed is the best a person can expect, that when it's time to go it's good to have the people you love in a circle around the bed, sad and nervous and maybe a little sick to their stomachs, but watching the dying man's face like it's about to break into sundown. Mr. Gene was practicing his deathbed way ahead of schedule, maybe not even practicing but some other kind of exercise you couldn't put a name to.

Mr. Gene tried to raise his head to answer my question but he was so far buried that he could only manage a nod or two, which I was grateful for. But after the tornado, practicing for his deathbed took a few different turns until one day he said he was done with it: *I've done all I can do,* he said. *The rest is up to the Lord.* This was just a few weeks ago, so he must have known somehow that the real thing was coming, and that it would find him way out here at the edge of this small town in Nebraska in the blind woman's house with the rough-looking characters who found us staring at him. And what more can you ask for than that—that when the time comes you're ready because you've done the best you can, practicing for your deathbed? When you think about it that way it makes a helluva lot of sense. In fact, you'd be hard put to make better use of your time, if you're lucky enough to find a bed that will accommodate you between this life and the next in white sheets like a sailboat as you slowly drift off into the sunset.

Munoz

I saw the bleeding calf look in Gus's and Oly's eyes, but fuck that overblown shit. Yarborough I didn't know about, but you never can tell about Y: he just kept his eyes on the blind lady, who sat there in the corner like she was carved out of glowing stone. They had a deep dark history between them that nobody else knew nothing about, so you learned to leave it well enough the fuck alone.

The preacher had his props and I had mine.

That's all I'm saying. And they weren't gonna cross wires anytime soon. Just when he finally kicked it for good I had to get away, that's all. So what if I had something in my eye so it looked like I was crying? Anything wrong with that? I don't gotta explain it to nobody, least of all the homies I grew up with. I paid my dues long ago, but it seems like I got to keep paying them over and over for hearing the preacher go on the way he did, like some fool going up and down the FM dial because he doesn't know what he wants to listen to.

I mean, here we salvage his Tropicana ass out near the reservoir and he goes supernova and pristine on us, saying how we were destined to listen to him at the end of his life and other crazy shit so I could hardly stand to listen to him, 'specially with Shindig waiting out in the truck bitching and moaning in my inner ear in whispers made of torched desert air.

I told Shindig in my mind to just chill out, bro, the worst's over by a long shot, so cut me a little slack while I watch the preacher die and then we can get on with what we talked about, flying home from the sandbox. I ain't gonna leave you hanging. But I knew Shindig and I knew he was out there pouting in the truck like somebody's lapdog: I could feel those disapproving vibes all the way inside in the blind lady's house with the rain coming down in droves.

Sometimes he's worse than a dick-deprived diva, Shindig is. But I told him, I promised him a long time ago that I got his back and that means forever, man. Sometimes I can't blame him for wanting extra reassurance because you don't find it very often in this world, especially after what he'd been through. He didn't have much of a clue when I first saw him, but why I have to keep on taking care of his sorry ass is beyond my comprehension.

So I wasn't having any charitable thoughts about the preacher dying in front of us. I'd seen all that shit before, enough people dead and dying to do a remake of Michael Jackson's "Thriller." I wasn't particularly interested in a preacher dying and shooting off his holy-rolling mouth in a made-up bed during a thunderstorm. Maybe my sympathy the world over had just been stretched too far and I only had enough left for Shindig. Because how he ended up in the Corps I'll never know. Some promises you end up regretting later on, but a promise is a fucking promise, so it don't make much difference how you feel about it one way or the other, and that's exactly where I found myself, back in the blind lady's house.

So, yeah, I had a lot on my mind. And preacher man wasn't high on my list of priorities. I'd been back just a month or so, and I was still dragging my feet over what I promised to do for Shindig. I was procrastinating big time and, to tell the truth, I don't even know why. Shindig wasn't gonna cause me any problems. I guess I had just gotten used to his lame-ass company. It happens sometimes, you know, like Tom Hanks in the movie *Cast Away* when he gets attached to that volleyball and can't let it go, no matter how weird it seems to the outside world.

But the preacher man just kept going on and on, like a ventriloquist's dummy jacked up on steroids. Maybe if he'd been a priest I would have listened a little better, but that's probably just another head fuck I'm trying on for size. I figure if you're dying and you *know* you're dying, then just die and spare the rest of us. I know that doesn't sound very sympathetic, but like I said, I'd seen so many go down before who hardly said a word, glassy eyes staring down the great cosmic suckhole that there's nothing about death the preacher could tell me that I hadn't seen already from the vantage point of a smoking Humvee. It wasn't like we were under fire, just standing there while it rained outside like kids in a classroom where the lessons were being taught by a talking mannequin in a fucked-up funhouse.

If it's your time then I say commence that ultimate shit in the shadow of the valley of death eclipsing everything you know. Don't waste other people's time because they might be wanting more pussy or to plant a garden or go skydiving or some other shit like that.

Hey, Shindig, man—you hear what this preacher says?

That he's dying for us?

What do you think of that, Shin?

Think this shit's for real?

But Shindig, he don't know nothing anymore but the promise you made, *Munoz, promise me,* his ears unable to pick up any other message. He could use a little humor, Shindig could, always needed some. That's been his lifelong dilemma in the first place, right up to where he is now. When he first got there I said to myself, *You fucking kidding me?* Give me something to work with, Uncle Sam. But sometimes Sam isn't too discriminating. Since the first day I saw him I've been looking out for Shindig, and it's been a full-time job without pay, man, 24-7.

Even though I didn't owe the preacher a goddamned thing and there was no reason to stand there and listen to him go on, I ended up listening to every word he said to the bitter end, and I don't even know why, man.

And Shindig was out there waiting for me. I was trying to balance one ying with the other yang, trying to do the right thing, only the right thing was two things at the same time, so what's it gonna be? There was the preacher and his psychedelic talk show with rose petals falling down, and then there was Shindig waiting for me out in the truck like an altar boy in the first row, glowing with the light pouring in from the stained-glass windows in rays of glory.

I was caught between two worlds, and when the preacher finally died, I don't know, the sudden silence in the room and all of us just standing there got to me all at once and I had to get out of there, not only because it was the end of his life but for what we did in the blind lady's house all those years ago.

I thought the preacher was 99 percent full of shit, telling us he had picked us out from some divine lineup in the sky. We just found the dude a few hours before. And the girl was sitting there at the end of the bed, keeping her eyes on him all the way, and I was thinking, *Why do I have to see and hear this now with Shindig waiting for me out in the truck?* We'd come such a long way, over mountains and valleys and the Euphrates River, with tracers lighting up the sky and the death of brothers who went down fighting or holding what was left of their faces for that fucked-up idea of a war that spiraled out of control till we just had each other.

Preacher cast a spell on me is what he did, hypnotized me with his voodoo mouth. When he was dead I snapped out of it and realized all the things I'd lost and would never get back again. It hit me all at once, like a flood sweeping me out into the ocean, so much that had gone wrong I didn't know where to start or how to add it all up, yours truly in the middle reaching out but not able to hold on to a god-damned thing. I thought of Vietnam and Korea and World

War II and the other wars I'd heard about and I didn't want to believe it was just for nothing, man, oil or some other political maneuver, but that's what it was once you cut away all the bullshit. And Shindig waiting for me out in the truck, not making a sound, patient as Mount Rushmore, because I'd made him a promise I couldn't go back on.

I loved him.

That's what it boils down to—I loved that towheaded, hopeless motherfucker. You took one look at him with a weapon in his hands and you thought, Man, there's something wrong with this picture: he should be studying accounting at some Podunk college watching Seinfeld reruns at night, getting hard under his desk and trying to fight off lustful thoughts about the stacked chick next to him.

But not here. Not over here.

First time I saw him, I thought, This is some fucked-up shit to have a kid like him out here, watching him lag behind everyone else on every routine thing, lacing up his boots at the speed of a slow-motion dream.

Hey, Shindig, you wanna hurry up so we can get on with what we gotta do here?

Sir, yes, sir—

But it didn't help him get it done any faster. He was the most suspect marine I ever knew, so I took it upon myself to look out for him while at the same time riding his ass as hard as I could to keep him out of harm's way, which I know is in violation of every code there is. But I didn't care anymore. Anyone who messed with Shindig had to mess with me, so they learned to leave him alone.

Nobody hated Shindig so much as they were afraid of what would happen if they got too close to him. He did the best he could with what he had, but it wasn't worth jack shit. And everybody knew it. That's it, that's all it was, like Shindig was radioactive under his clothes, more likely to go up in a ball of flames because he just wasn't cut out for it.

Why couldn't somebody see that before, is what I wanna know?

Why couldn't someone see this kid and just admit there was no way you were gonna mold him into the man-eater you wanted?

Why, man?

What was so awful about admitting the truth?

I'm talking the big picture, man, the one that creeps into your mind after you've seen others go down and the sudden appearance of a doofus like Shindig who comes fresh out of Dreamland, USA. The very first day I caught him in the head, whacking off to a picture of his girlfriend and crying like a baby, his half-hard dick in his hand like one of those inflatable elves you see in people's front yards around Christmas. I just walked up to him and grabbed the picture out of his hand but he kept right on going, working his meat over like he was trying to raise the dead.

Don't start feeling sorry for yourself already, Shindig,

I said and he just covered himself up with one hand and reached out for the picture with the other. I looked at his Mary Beth, and she was good-looking, no doubt about it, about seventeen or eighteen. I wondered how she ended up with someone like Shindig and decided it had to be because he didn't pose no radical threat to her homecoming queen status, though one day she'd get tired of his squeaky clean ways and find somebody else. She had bleach-blonde hair and perfect white teeth, like a life-sized Barbie doll.

And Shindig didn't say nothin', just looked up at me with his hand reaching out with little boy tears coming down his imploring eyes—and at that moment, I mean right then, like light pouring out of the sky, I thought of a picture of Jesus I'd seen once when I was eight years old: a picture out of a book my mother gave me, Jesus praying in the garden before they came and crucified his ass, with rays of light coming down from heaven all around but no signs of rescue or angels on the way, no one in the world who was gonna stop the nails that were coming to pound through his hands and feet, not even God himself. Shindig looked just like this picture-book Jesus, like they were identical twins minus a halo around Shindig's head, only he was reaching out with one hand while the other was covering his dick—but the expression was the same exact one dead on, and it was just eerie, man, like déjà vu all over again and the sign of the apocalypse rolled into one, and I handed back his cavity-free Mary Beth to spunk over, but I don't think he could get it up again to full mast and that was just as well because we were moving out in half an hour.

And I walked out of that head spooked out of my gourd, man.

I hadn't thought of that picture for years, didn't even realize I remembered it until I saw Shindig's face looking up at me. Jesus hardly ever meant anything to me but rules and more rules and Sister Calista, who smelled like furniture polish, but I swear it was like Jesus trying to get off on a picture of his girlfriend before we went out on patrol. Shindig was the weak link in the chain, man, the one nobody wanted to be around because he'd be the one to fuck up somewhere down the line—and nobody wanted to be around him when he did. After a week they didn't even try to hide it anymore, just pariahed him day after day in subtle ways, no way you could even notice it unless you knew what was going on.

Enson called it the Shindig Zone, and that zone got a little bigger each day. A few inches here, a few inches there, shit like that. There was nothing nobody could do about it, just a fact of life and death and survival of the fittest. I got exactly what I bargained for, so there isn't any reason to pity me or call me hero even with my Purple Heart because I went into it looking for action, and that's exactly what I got.

But Shindig, Corey PF-fucking-C Shindig—he threw that scenario right out the window. I asked him once,

Shindig, why'd you sign up for this shit, clean-cut Wyoming boy like you?

And he just looked at me all bashful and shy, embarrassed almost, and said,

I want to pay for school myself because my parents can't afford it.

Ever heard of student loans, man?

But he wanted to pay his own way. He said it would mean more to him if he paid his own way, that it was the right thing to do. What can you say to that? He saw himself and Mary Beth getting a huge white house and breeding a flock of little Shindigs to live happily ever after.

The American Dream, man, the American Dream. I've heard it all before: it's got people seeing stars and stripes in their sleep and twenty-four-hour shopping malls with every flavor under the sun. They don't see the black eyes of the Iraqi girl who looked like my niece Frieda, going into shock after I shot her during a raid. Don't dream me no American Dream, man, cause you can't have the dream without the nightmare. Shindig was like the last true believer, holding onto it longer than anybody else. But he asked me to make him a promise. *Promise me, O. Promise me.* He'd had a premonition that he was going down, he was haunted by his own death, walking around on a gangplank that went all the way to the Persian Gulf. *Promise me, O. You gotta do that for me.* So that's what it boiled down to after all was said and done, a promise you make that you just gotta keep no matter what.

But still I listened to the preacher the whole time for a reason I'll never understand: I stood there hour after hour letting him talk his deathbed rap with Shindig waiting out in the truck for me. And that will always be a mystery to me, that this goofy-ass preacher could come out of nowhere and tell us how it is and what we've been avoiding for so long. I'll never understand that as long as I live. But the other part of it was that it gave me a little extra time with Shindig, made me think we could just keep driving across the country, swapping war stories all the way up to Alaska till the cash ran out and I finally had to make good on what he had asked me to do.

Truth was, me and Shindig had a lot of unfinished business, shit we needed to work out before I followed through. I'd been telling him that ever since we got back, but it seemed like he only had ears for what we already talked about. But I wanted to get to the bottom of what happened that day in Fallujah, what he thought he was trying to prove when we were cut off from air support for more than two hours.

They set a trap for us, man, and we were so intent on nailing their asses we drove right into it. Then when the dust cleared we were just sitting ducks out there, exposed as you can be at an intersection, after we tripped some mines. Seemed like everybody was shooting at us then, little kids with handguns, women with head scarves, old men with prayer beads throwing hand grenades. We weren't even supposed to be there in the first place. After they about blew us all to hell they suddenly stopped firing and there was this voice over a P.A. system usually used for Ezan. Mussa, the Iraqi guide we had with us, said they'd take one of us and let the rest of us go. But they wanted one of us. Clarkson had already bled to death, Aikens had broken eardrums and couldn't hear a goddamned thing, and nobody was coming anytime soon to help us. We were cut off and exposed. I thought they'd burn us alive and drag our corpses through the streets or string them up from the nearest fucking bridge.

One marine, Mussa said, they want one marine. Then the rest of us can go, they swear on the heads of their children.

We look at each other, just the six of us left,

me, Shindig, Owens, Michaels, and Mussa, with Aikens deaf as a post and going into shock and Clarkson dead on the floor in a pool of blood. And before anyone could say anything, before anyone could hardly move, Shindig got up and started climbing out of the Humvee waving his hand. I tried to pull him back down but the skinny fucker kicked me in the face. He took the decision-making process right out of our hands, man, before anyone could even say a word.

He gets out without his weapon and his arms held high above his head into the noonday heat and starts walking to where the voice is coming from, but it was like the voice of God because it was coming from everywhere. We just watched him walk away. They start cheering, you can hear them happy as hell that they have their American, that he comes out easy as you please.

One of them shoots him in the arm and spins him around until he does this little drunken pirouette into the sand, sitting down and cradling it with his good arm. He's about sixty meters away. And nobody moves, it's so quiet. *Shindig!* I yell, *Shindig!* But he doesn't look up at me, just cradles his arm like it's a broken toy sitting there Indian-style. I should have shot him right then, two shots to the chest, two to the head, like I'd been trained, but I don't. I hardly know what the fuck's happening. All I know is that Shindig has walked out alone and unarmed, becoming the scapegoat for the rest of us. *Dangit,* I hear him say. *Dangit.* But it's like he's all alone out there with nobody around for hundreds of miles, Shindig and his bleeding arm sitting in the middle of a deserted intersection.

Why didn't I shoot you, Shindig?

Why didn't I lock down on you and end it right there?

We're sitting there in the Humvee watching him, and he's already so far away, already becoming the memory that would haunt us for the rest of our lives.

What was it like out there, Corey?

Can you tell me?

Can you forgive me for not being the one, for

not moving fast enough?

Corey?

They come out of the bombed out buildings covered from head to foot with just a slit for eyes, holding their AKs around their hips and pointed at Shindig, and we don't know what the fuck to do. They move like one person, like they've choreographed it a hundred times. The loudspeaker comes on again and Mussa won't tell us what it's saying, just lowers his head and starts praying to Allah.

Tell us what he's saying, Mussa. Tell us what the fuck's going on.

But he won't look at us. All we can do is watch from the smoking Humvee, all we can do is wait for our own birds to come swooping in.

Now they're almost at Shindig, surrounding him in a semi-circle: one of them raises his AK and fires a round into the air. A cheer goes up again, but it's like the whole neighborhood cheers with one Arab mouth, one cry, one victory shout for the whole Middle East. Shindig sits there looking at his arm, like he hasn't even noticed them yet. The loudspeaker gets louder and I grab Mussa by the shirt to tell us what the fuck is going on, but he won't look at me, won't open his eyes—and I push him back and look out again. A dude with a turban like an Italian tablecloth comes out of one of the buildings holding the longest sword I've ever seen, walking toward Shindig real slow and reverent-like, holding the sword with both hands as the crowd makes a gauntlet for him.

They're chanting for him, they're cheering for him, it's all happening like something out of a dream, and I aim my weapon but I don't take a shot, I don't for some reason, and Mussa's not helping at all, and I'm confused and clear-headed at the same time, and it's not happening this way, it can't be, but it is, and he's almost at Shindig now and Corey hasn't looked up and one of them grabs him by the shoulders and makes him kneel down and they're all pointing their AKs and grenade launchers at us and the loudspeaker's shrieking out the end of the world as we watch him lift the sword above Shindig's head and he looks at me, Shindig does, he looks at me but he doesn't see me, his eyes already glassed over like he's drunk, and I see the spit around his lips and maybe some sand and the blade comes down in a flashing arc and Shindig's head pops off like a cork with spurts of blood streaming out of the trunk of his body as it starts to keel over and his head rolls wide-eyed in the sand, looking at the sun until it comes to rest eight feet away from his body with the back of it facing us because it's too embarrassed, and I open fire but it's like they're already gone and Aiken is hit and Michaels goes down and Mussa's still down on the floor not looking at anything before the birds come and strafe the whole neighborhood in a river of rippling fire.

I gotta get Corey's head, I gotta get it for him, for me, for Mary Beth, for the whole fucking planet and kids eating Cheerios in Chicago—and under cover of those birds I crawl out there before the insurgents blow up the Humvee and I'm crawling toward Shindig's blond head now, making my way across the street with chaos flying all around, and I finally get to it.

Just me and you now, Corey.

You don't have to worry about anything.

Shindig's looking at me, and he even starts to smile and blinks once, then he's gone and I'm cradling his head.

Uncle Tito used to let me and my cousin Ricky watch him as he cut off the heads of chickens. Uncle Tito could hardly speak English and kept saying, *Lo siento por los pollos*, apologizing to the chickens. It was fun as kids to watch him cut the heads off and watch the body of the chicken run around in crazy eights pumping its cartoon legs. Some of them ran longer than others, and some didn't even seem to die at all except for the head Uncle Tito held in his hand, looking at us dazed and confused out of its chicken window eyes. There was nothing funnier or more pathetic than a chicken head, man, nothing you could have less respect for than a headless chicken and the way its body ran around like it was on fire. You couldn't have respect for a headless chicken, man. And that's why they did it. That's why they cut the heads off their enemies. Because it's worse than anything else you could think of, letting somebody's head roll around like that. *Lo siento por los pollos. Lo siento.* Sorry to the chickens, man.

Shindig's out in the truck waiting for me. I keep him in a bowling ball bag, but nobody knows it's him. I'm gonna take him back to his hometown in Wyoming. I promised him. I listened to the preacher as he was dying, and I could feel Shindig staring at me through the jar. *If I die you take me back to Wyoming, O. Promise me, O. Promise me.* I promise you, Corey. I promise. I'm not gonna let you down. I got so used to covering your ass anyway it's like a habit I can't kick.

But what made you do it, Corey?

I just want you to tell me that before I take you home. Please tell me your secret. The preacher's been talking rainbows and pussycats. He called us brides, man. I didn't look at Danny or Oly or Y—I don't have to. The blind lady is like a net of starfish, like a piece of glowing tin. *Lo siento, blind lady. Lo siento.* For what we did. How we broke in here.

I have a friend out in the truck and his name is Corey Shindig. He's from Casper, Wyoming, about five hours away from here. He's got this sweet-looking girlfriend named Mary Beth, who's waiting for him. She's been faithful the whole time he was away. They used to sit out on the porch: she wore a white summer dress and Shindig wore some Dockers and a pressed shirt. He was a real gentleman. He was gonna marry her, they were gonna settle down and have kids, he was gonna be a CPA and a soccer coach. He believed in God and country, he went into the Corps so he could pay for college, he was a good and loyal marine, and he gave his life up for me and for the others who didn't make it. The preacher says we come from the light and we're gonna return to it someday, that we're children of the light and it blesses us even in the darkest of days. He says we gotta marry the light like brides even though we're men. Corey would believe that. Corey would say it's true.

He's nodding out in the truck. I'm gonna take him home so he can finally rest in peace. But first I gotta ask him a few things. I wanna hear what he has to say. I'll be hanging on to every word, I'll be make sure I hear them right so I can make amends and know that what happened happened because it had to, and that's all there is to it, man, that's all anybody can say.

Twilight Song

The preacher moved his bare skinny legs back and forth to the beat of an unknown rhythm, metronome to a fatal countdown and his own feverish words that came crazed and madcap out of his spit-flecking mouth. The men, with their bloodshot eyes, were gathered around the bed while the girl sat at the foot of the bed near the Ground Zero of his dying. The blind woman in her spotless white shawl sat motionless in her rocking chair as a faint glow came rising off the delicate lace.

The preacher said he gave them peace in the garland of a sigh.

He said his skin would not infect them, only show them how it is, his nostrils soon to shudder in wheeze-flaps of forever.

He said dark comes slender now and that all anybody could do was suffer it.

He asked them was it worth it, who you are and what you've

done and haven't done in slow retrogrades of a berserker's clutch and carry, leaving only the soot of ashes?

He told them to remember bright trees touching forever, that the will of acres is flowering and the will of sky is staring.

And they listened despite themselves, enraptured, enraged, and unaccountably moved, especially the one who kept trying to stifle his pent-up laughter. None of them could explain how they came to be in the blind woman's house or why the preacher was talking the way he was—why they were called and summoned to witness the tail end of his dying and what they were supposed to do in the wake of his outrageous avowals.

Three hours into the deathwatch the one they called O. slipped out of the house and came back twenty minutes later, his face wet and streaming with rain. He settled back into the vigil as if he had never left. The big one covered in tattoos hardly moved at all, while the other tall one wearing cowboy boots worn down to the heels kept looking at the blind lady, who continued to sit in her chair like a force field unto herself that kept pulling his hungry eyes. The girl who had been hauling the wagon full of bibles sat at the foot of the bed as if she'd seen the preacher laid up like that before, only this time it was different, off the charts for ultimacy and bona fide.

Lightning flashed periodically into the windows of the tiny house, taking snapshots of the room, preserving in the postures and expressions of a lifetime in stark daguerreotypes rocketing across the far-reaching plains, the glistening cogs of the preacher's mouth working overtime and pogoing out leaflets of spit like the transparent scales of a hornet's wing. He managed to beguile them in droves of improbable speech as if the fading lights of his failing body were all gathered together in a single invisible chord or current and came streaming out of his mouth in a cataract of pleadings, pledges, and endearments filling up the claustrophobic air.

He tried once to rise up on his elbows to let loose another freestyle aphorism, only to fall back in a heap of oomph as the girl bowed and shook her head, letting out a grief-stricken whimper. Outside the rain had commenced to turn to hail and come down in the timpani of bouncing golf balls, the blind lady's roof tumbling over with the roiling downpour from a thunderhead ten miles wide. Framed in the outlines of a window the blind lady gave birth time and time again to a rapt stillness that sang out of the air whenever the lightning struck, herself illumined and radiated by the intricate lace of her handmade shawl, which sang of other storms and sittings, other deep auditions that kept returning to the heart of a boundless mystery. So it was not just the dying and ranting preacher who commanded the men's attention, or even the girl's; the blind lady became the silent and lit-up foil that gave the preacher's words added impetus and urgency like quicksilver arabesques carving up the air.

Each smelled the lightning after it struck in telltale wafts of cordite and dripping stones hauled up from a riverbed, taking them back to a time and place where every light was one, before the preacher brought them back with the lassoed tremolo of his quavering voice circling around their inmost revelations. So they stood or sat watching and listening to the preacher sink deeper into dying as the storm raged on in rife *tinkles of catastrophic glass, and they did not turn away nor shut their ears against the incantations he had prepared for them, the blind lady set off and isolated from the rest, giving the preacher's dying its own dimly lit cloud with the glowing seeds of forbearance in it.*

Marian

That night I heard them like a wave of tumbling sand coming from far away, a dry high-up sound carrying nothing in its wake but the frail coats of dead hornets crackling in the air. I always knew they'd come, a whole lifetime in the knowing going back to sunlight and a hand reaching down to touch me. I'd run my fingers carefully over the edges of this knowledge like they were so many sawteeth sticking out of the ground.

You make yourself believe that destruction will pass you over, like a wind on its way to somewhere else, that you can accept it somehow. Go somewhere where it's safe. You do this sometimes, trick yourself into believing it. But it doesn't work that way. The light comes and goes and you feel it best when it is brightest, when you know it's there like a swarm of messages trying to tell you something. But what is it? What is the light trying to tell you? Only that you'll live forever, is all:

that whatever is inside of you knows the light even if you are blind and will return to it someday. So call it ignorance, call it heartbreak—call it whatever you want. It doesn't matter what you call it anyway. Destruction can't touch it, or harm it in any way—and this is the real truth on top of the lie you keep telling yourself, that you'll be unmarked, that you'll be secure and left alone, that these terrible things will pass you by because you are exempt somehow.

That's why I knew those boys were coming to do what they did.

They were like puppets on a string, like all destroyers are, a part of that same oncoming sound, that driving, the headlights I couldn't see sweeping across my walls. They were coming for me less to hurt me than to act out something they thought they had to do, the ongoing mystery of violence that still does not have a cure as long as there are young men who have something to prove. Long before they got here I felt them coming in the veins of my body, carrying the sound of the sea and light motes so small they trembled like bits of glowing ember, the spatula walls of my heart they wanted to violate and the kingdom of my innards where bread turns into breathing. They were there, they were always there, coming over the horizon in the hunkered stares of pheasants hiding in the grass and the changing of the seasons, the death of my parents, the death of my son, my husband, the ash crop of my dried-up tears.

Marian, someone told me, this is what you have to do: this is what you have to be in order for it to pass through. So I learned to wait for them each evening, sitting in the chair Bud made for me, wearing a shawl made of spiderwebs, waiting for the lights like a warm singing breeze against my skin.

And for what?

To come into my home with me sitting here alone, to spray paint the walls and smash up the furniture and keepsakes of my life, ceramic cups hand-made in Colorado so many feet above sea level and the pictures of my son I couldn't see, to take me into the bedroom and take off my clothes like he was digging out a tomb—to believe, because I'm old and blind, that I'm defenseless, that whatever you're about to do you do because you can so there's no reason to question why because I'm like a magnet pulling at you as you come with meathooks in your eyes and the smell of lighter fluid on your fingertips. Yes, I know about these, all the wayward ways, the weather signs of your arrival. I heard you coming for years. The waiting makes you gentle and the waiting makes you strong and goes on longer than you ever thought it would, past your body and your life, never stopping, your mouth heaped with sadness in the empty twilight where every cry is pure.

Yes, I know—can't be any other way.

Your headlights blossom over the shelf of the world and I waited for you each night, my face feeling those beams mapped against it like the x-rays of a dead man's teeth, where I sat caught up like a candle flame in the headlights, not moving—not because I'm brave but because I've waited all this time and you're almost here to turn off the music and stumble out of your truck in ritual damnation, to reel back on your heels where drunkenness takes your head like a storm before you throw up in the weeds. I'm not going anywhere.

I learned to forgive you long before you ever touched me.

I've felt the light falling on children's faces, where the sun meets their skin from a million miles away and abandoned barns sluice-gated for rays of thin desiring and the echo of hay takes over in golden shafts that shudder the broken roofs. And the twilight beggary of my surrender, where the light comes inching up my body each day so I can see it with my skin, learning to wait all over again as if I've never waited for anything, myself like a broken sundial that ran out of time long ago remembering back to Buddy playing in the backyard where I could not see him but felt his moving body, knowing he would have to leave me but not knowing when. Each day was a church I crawled into on my hands and knees, right up to the altar of his burning death that took him away, the thing I could never tell Bud because he wouldn't understand. I would not do that to him. It would be cruel to tell him if he couldn't understand how I knew that I knew it and how the knowledge bled me before it happened.

And the light on Buddy's casket after the accident, where they tried to put back the little that was left of him a few days before his twenty-ninth birthday, the light like a frail blond drape dragging across our grief. And light pouring out of people's mouths when they tried to say something nice—I was already moving far away so that I seemed to overhear them like strangers talking down the street, not in words, just the familiar sound of voices, the cracks of their lips and you don't have to say it, please, there aren't any words, but they said it anyway, light inside their coffee-smelling mouths so meager you could wipe the table with it. To put him in the ground, to bury him so that the light can't reach him except through the gumming of worms, the burying of him, not blindness but darkness unto darkness, lid-fitted for the groping of dream hands.

Bud didn't know what to do with his hands after Buddy died, so he put them to work fixing whatever he could, things that weren't even broken—plaster in the walls and bricks in the chimney, creating jobs that would keep his hands busy from what he was afraid would happen if they were still, the sob rising in his throat threatening to blot out everything he knew and believed in. They fluttered in front of him like restless birds flying up from the ground, and I knew what it was, though I couldn't say it: not just Buddy's death but how was he supposed to go on after it, which was not something he was ever prepared to deal with because his son was supposed to take up where he left off and that's all there was to it.

I couldn't tell him what I knew.

So his hands washed over me at night, feeling less for love than searching to make sure I was there, so it was almost like Bud was the blind one as he felt my body for what meanings he thought were written in the hollows of my knees and my heels, which he held in each hand like he was choosing between stones, down into my womanhood, where he fished with his fingers beyond my cries and cheekbones, traced with his callused thumbs, trying to read them and make sense of them, over and over the ritual of his searching hands wanting proof past what I could tell him and not tell him, that Buddy was gone and that's all we knew for sure, that we couldn't bring him back no matter how we tried, that he was a good boy who grew into something wild we never could have imagined, and that's part of the loss and the forgiveness, the forgiveness of ourselves, that we were still alive and our restless son was dead.

I gotta make sure you're still there

you said, and I kept still in the dark because there was nothing left to say. Let the father grieve in his way, clutching at whatever he can put a hand to. Let him point with the divining rods of his shaking fingers which way the fallen apples are. Because grief makes us strangers even to ourselves, searching for how it fits together, though it's not for anyone to know or understand—how your own child can go before you into the ground and haunt your days and nights, saying things you never heard, in a voice becoming a faint, amber echo with yearning dripping all over it like honey.

I'd get out of bed at night and sit at the kitchen table wrapped up in a shawl I made myself: there's so much you can't share with another person, I'm surprised you can share anything. I became expert at crying in the dark and choking back the sound, muffling my cries and swallowing my sobs so it almost felt like contractions or getting sick in the morning. My tears did my seeing for me, falling like pieces of broken glass, sprinkling lights wherever they landed. I thought I'd get used to it but I never did—thought if I cried enough I'd somehow get over the fact that Buddy died before us, but

I should have known I was fooling myself. But there was nothing to pity me for, now or then, no need to say or think anything with the word sorry in it. Just was, just is.

Most nights I'd sit at the kitchen table past midnight, listening to the chimes on the porch ringing *save me, save me* and I'd be lost to their wind-driven songs that were never the same but still familiar somehow, just out of reach, chimes that seemed to take in every other sound and making it a part of them, the scraping of a chair or branch clawing at the window, my sighs and sobs rising like sails, but it was just me at the tail end of everything hollowed out for the sound that was like every sound there was or could be, Bud's band saw whining in the garage, Buddy's laughter in the hallway, my own hands at some new gingham fabric I was stitching into a pattern—all kinds of separate sounds ending up in the chimes at night, where I sat and listened after the crying went through me and drew me into shivers. I'd hear the chimes my sister Frances gave me and come to believe that even if the world was to end those chimes would still somehow make their music out of nothing, so it was the purest, simplest thing there ever was or could be.

Bud would be snoring in the bedroom, or turning over in the rough, impatient way he used to do, muttering his dream hopes out loud, and I'd feel my life turning into something quiet and almost serene in the double dark knowing it was past midnight out in the country with farm lights separating the miles like pieces from a broken chandelier I remembered seeing when I was a girl. Then Buddy's death was not the awfulest thing ever but one of those terrible

things that just had to happen and that you learn to live
with because that's the way it is and it can't be otherwise.
Only once did Bud ever wake up and call for me, but I think
he was half-asleep because he didn't mention it and didn't
make much sense.

Marian? Marian?

I'm out in the kitchen, Bud. I'll be in in a little bit.

Okay, then. Mind the caraway seeds in the sink,
he said.

Then quiet, then the chimes again. Bud called me a tiny
little thing and I guess I've always been. Small enough, he
said, to put away in a drawer on a rainy day.

Sometimes after crying I believed every drought was
false because I was living proof of the water inside all of us,
never to abate. All you got to do is cry. And one night, falling
somewhere between sleep and half-sleep, my tears drenched
the front of my body and dripped off my fingers. I got up
and went to the window—not because I could look but to
know the seeing was there outlined like a stamp, framing
the heaped-up distance: over the corn, the hills rising in the
distance, the clouds, the China-chipped moon.

I was foolish then, am no doubt foolish still.

But Buddy. Buddy. I remember the smell of you when
you were five years old, the needles of your hair sticking up
after sleep, the way you slouched into the kitchen early in the
morning, never saying much, moping over your breakfast
while your father went about whistling, scrubbed and ready
to work, in lock-step with the roustabout world.

You were my son, but you were given to us just for a little

while. I counted the days by scratching them under the table with a knife—

some with spaces between them like tooth marks, feeling the grooves with my fingers at night so I could feel the hollowness growing in me like thorns, my secret way to mark you.

Why would I mark you under the table, Buddy?

It was a silly thing to do, like I was trying to keep you from going away. When they broke in I knew they wouldn't touch them, wouldn't even know they were there, and that gave me something, that secret knowledge, those marks I took care of all those years.

One night God let me see you, Buddy, as a weeping willow tree on fire and I saw you trembling, lemon-heat in my mind, so many spokes of wheeling light and drifting ash, each one like a mouth saying, *Help me*, but I couldn't. I never could and that was my helplessness, the shaking wires of your hair singing up and down like a horse. You were a tree with the lights rocking in it Buddy and that was your soul, how you grew up into the sky with nothing to protect you with cleared empty space all around for miles. When I talk to you the world goes silent except for the chimes, and I can't remember your father's voice and this makes me ashamed.

Because how can you forget the voice of the man you loved?

I remember nursing you, Buddy, the veins inside your head pulsing to the drinking you made of me, your tiny fingers clutched around my breast and the smell of us together, lint from the laundry and the smell of your clean-washed baby's hair. There was dust swimming in the corner of the room but I didn't care. I cried with you in my arms, my tears washing down over your face while you emptied me, taking a paler light with you down the drains of your body. You were greedy, Buddy, you were always greedy, but I don't know what good it is to know that now, to remember like I do and talk like you're still alive.

When I'm dead I'll see past the burning tree you were to me, rocking in cradles of light. Your father, I can't say. I don't know about him. He shows up in the big, vivid things of this world, ready to bust wide open. It's this hunch I have, a feeling that comes in a shiver and a draft under the door. I wish he'd let me go. Maybe in death you could tell him that. I can't talk to him like I can to you.

Bud, I'd say, you're gonna have to let us go because the more you hug us to yourself the faster the earth spins and keeps things chained to the ground and that's how gravity works, even when they came that night in their headlights scanning the walls. I don't know how my waiting turned into something else, but I became a part of the moon and the sky and said to myself, *They're coming, they're almost here.* You're a blind old woman who lives alone and makes dolls out of discarded things and you're used to talking to your dead son because his ears are made of hollowed-out shells waiting for the light, and one day peace arrives with the taste of glowing seeds in it and Lord precious light feeding you in the dark silence of your waiting as the walls of your house become hands folded in prayer and that is all. That is everything.

A few days before they came I had an errand to run and it was far away in town, about seven miles away. I knotted seventy-seven skeins of yarn together at 185 yards each and tied the end of them around my waist. Then I got seventy-some beanpoles that I would use as stakes every 200 yards or so to keep the yarn from getting tangled up. I'd count off while I went. I remember thinking this would be my one adventure and then I could be done with it: whatever was going to happen would, so I should do what I had in mind to do.

I walked out of the house on a hot August morning toward Point Blank. I aimed to get there by myself. You see this blind woman walking down a country road with a string of yarn trailing behind her and my, it's almost like you're tied to her and everyone else who sees her and even those who don't. Even though it was hot I wore the shawl I had made myself, which glowed in the dust in bright pockets of air. I could feel them around me gathering. I kept up a good pace but I didn't walk too fast as the dirt of the road brushed against me and came up whispering against my knees. I shuffled along and my footsteps made a clear scraping sound that made me think of churning oats and the shucking of corn. There was no need to hurry. If the yarn broke, why, then, I was lost. But I didn't worry about it. The yarn would hold me.

Bud liked to have me in the house where he knew where I was, though I knew I'd walk away someday and wouldn't have to explain it to anybody. I wasn't out to prove anything, but there was something I had to get and I wanted to get it myself without help from anyone.

I got the idea of tying myself to the house from old people who told stories of the Dust Bowl and how they couldn't see for the churning air, then coughing up buckets of dirt. That's what I'll do, I thought then, the first time I heard it: tie myself to the house with miles of yarn and spool it out walking into town. You have this yarn and it's a good strong yarn, called Lamb's Pride, and it will hold you and not break, lighting the way behind you like a string of light because that is exactly what it is.

I knew this other light once, this bright, gentle light stippling through the slats of Daddy's barn up near the hayloft with a window shining piles of straw where I sat for hours as a girl and no one knew where I was, a hushed, flooding light coming through spokes, splinters of wood high above in the shape of folded hands. I'd climb into the loft and close my eyes, sitting there letting the light fill me up to the brim of my forehead.

I called the light Glory Be and I think it was a good name to call it, Glory Be. I talked to Glory Be like you'd talk to your best friend, and it was and always would be.

Glory Be, how did you ever know how to find me here?

The girl knows better than the old woman why she had to ask it and why it can't be answered. God gives you pieces of light for the day when you can't see anymore, and why he does this I don't know but I don't begrudge it any. I saw Glory Be in my mind walking down the road and I can see it now, Glory Be holding me in a barn made of sunlight.

Mama would ring the bell and tears would start up in my eyes, but they weren't sad tears.

Glory Be, I'd whisper, tell me what it's like—

And the bell so mellow ringing over the fields as I took a piece of hay and stuck it between my teeth, sucking on it as hard as I could, taking Glory Be into my mouth and lungs, drinking it down to the nethermost, wise, dangerous child who knew what she was made of but not where it would lead her or who she would lose along the way. Mama's waving the dinner bell past the last booming mile, white of her arm flashing like a piece of cloud, and you could see the worried look on her face getting on to haggard with a wisp of damp hair across her forehead from the heat of the kitchen like a branch dragged through water.

> *Glory Be, tell me what the sun is saying*
> *past Mama's waving arm.*
> *Don't you know someone ringing a bell can't*
> *help saying yes to everything there*
> *is, even if it's sad and broken?*

But there was no answer to these questions—just the supper bell ringing in a drawn-out veil over the fields and Mama's hand waving it, the loose flap of her arm like a rug getting whacked in the yard.

Glory Be came back to me out on the road, and then I saw Buddy dying all over again, trapped in the grain elevator as clouds of grain caught fire and the dust exploded. I was looking down from the top of it like a weather vane and no matter how I tried I couldn't touch him, my hands fluttering around me like bits of burning paper. I sat up in bed and Bud asked what was wrong. All I could say was, *Buddy,*

Buddy, but I could hardly get his name out for the shaking tremors of it.

Buddy was working the night shift at Falco Grains—had been for about six months. It was all he could get at the time, temp work cleaning out the tunnels. He came home each day smelling like dead rats and flour. Three days before he died he told me he was quitting and moving away. He'd had a terrible fight with Bud. I never told Bud what Buddy said that day. Later I got the tape Buddy made for me, which I've memorized word for word so that sometimes I wake up in the middle of the night reciting it.

But that night I saw him dying in the fire and there was nothing I could do, looking down his screaming mouth to the roots of his throat where the fire grew, leaves around his head, saw him burning down where no one could help him, falling away from me, nothing I could do but stand at the top of it, watching it happen as the eyes of my heart drained into the night.

How can you see it if you're blind and fourteen miles away? I don't know the reasons or why I could see clouds of grain so stark and clear in my mind rushing up at me on updrafts of searing air with his mouth down in the middle of it like a baby bird waiting for food, but no, Buddy, you were no baby bird or I would have fed you: it was just the scream, the sound you made coming up at me and I couldn't do anything about it.

Bud tried to hold me, telling me it was just a dream, but I said he had to drive over there right away or call the Fire Department, but he wouldn't listen to me.

Marian, there's no reason—
You gotta get him out, he's trapped in there—

I saw Buddy's screaming mouth 120 feet down in the elevator, the rest of him engulfed in flames, and I'm at the top looking down, but the fire is not burning me as it rushes up licking the concrete sides, turning them into blackened bones.

When your son dies a violent death you are with him at the end for the rest of your life, reliving the agony and the fear because this is what a mother is. And you hear the screaming and sounds of fire consuming him, and he's stripped away past your ability to buffer it, and there's no other glass to see through because you are there in the heat going up in flames with your son who had to burn because that's the price you pay for loving him, never knowing what he looked like because you were blind before he was born. I talk to God about it each day, telling him to quick, melt him, turn his bones into soup and scald his eyes into vapor, the screams from his throat feeding the trembling church of the heated air, and God had to hear me because I told him so. I said it in front of Bud and when I was by myself. I said it like so much matter-of-fact discussion that it had to end with an agreement.

And other requests, demands even. Bud had to listen to me, and so did God. But on the night of Buddy's death Bud just tried to calm me down until I started to thrash in his arms to do something about it. Why won't you listen to what I'm saying? He's right here, burning up in front of us. Later, when he drove out and saw the smoke with his own eyes, he knew that Buddy was dead. There was hardly a body left to bury, just some teeth and bones, but Bud wanted him buried in a casket anyway.

I drew a picture of Buddy after he died to show Bud what he looked like to me, but I know I didn't get him right. Bud said he had crystal blue eyes and I believed him. I could see my son's soul and to me it was a candle flame standing in the doorway, Glory Be shining through the barn. Ashes from heaven, that's what you are to me now, Buddy. Now I take your voice into every room I walk into, hearing it even as I walked into town tied to my house by those skeins of yarn to get what I needed. I can hear you even now.

I keep the memory of your voice like some people carry snapshots in their wallets or put pictures on the walls or in frames on the bureau or next to their beds. It's all I have. I recorded him on the tape machine Bud bought for me because I asked him and I've played it ever since to hear his voice so that I will never not hear him talking to me.

Bud died five months to the day after Buddy died. Had a heart attack out in the field. Norm Steinkuhler found him next to the combine, thirty acres out. But I don't think he died of a heart attack. I think he died of a broken heart. I've wondered ever since if maybe I should have let him hear the tape, but there was something in me that said No, that tape wasn't meant for his ears. So he didn't know that Buddy was planning on leaving. Didn't know that he would have gone away three days later if he had lived. I never told him. I let him think that Buddy was considering staying on, doing all the things Bud dreamed for him; I let him have the comfort of those dreams even though they weren't true and now I wonder if all dreams aren't like that, especially the dreams we have for the ones who have to go away.

I listened for the sound of Buddy's laughter in the wind when I was walking into town with that bright stringing yarn trailing behind me, keeping me tied to the house. He had this desperate, cackling laugh—sometimes it sounded like crying. I figured on a good ten miles if it didn't get snagged or cut on something. Tied a double knot of it to the post of the front porch and then I was off.

Just a few cars passed by, and one of them stopped and asked if I was okay.

Just going into town for some medicine,

I told the driver, Don't worry about me. I'll be all right.

But I could tell he was concerned. Folks can be very considerate that way. I could feel him watching me in the rearview mirror as he drove off real slow. I must have been quite a sight, this little old blind lady walking on the side of the road with bright yarn trailing miles behind her.

I wondered what it looked like, I wondered if that single piece of string looked like a thread of light stretched across the whole world. I wasn't uppity about myself, but I did think, *Well, you don't ever have to feel that you're stuck, Marian.* I was surprised how good it felt out in the open like that, almost like a birthday.

But I lied to that driver. I wasn't going into town for any medicine. I knew those boys were coming before long, so

I wanted to get something. It was a funny little thing to want that couldn't make much of a difference one way or the other once they came: they'd still follow through on what they planned to do. It sounds so silly now, downright indulgent.

I remembered them from when I was a girl: must have been at least fifty years. When I was a girl, lemon drops were somehow sacred to me—and in my heart of hearts I didn't even call them lemon drops, but something else: I called them sun drops because I was convinced they were little drops of the sun, and every time I put one in my mouth it made my body and my whole face glow and then I was a little closer to Glory Be.

Even after I went blind I knew I had swallowed those pieces of light and I told myself they were growing inside me all this time and would have to shine out someday. That's how I thought of it then and think of it now. Those boys couldn't take that from me, my son's and husband's death couldn't, all those years living by myself couldn't.

Why, nothing the world over could, then or ever.

When I finally made it into town I asked this nice young woman where the drugstore was, and she walked me right up to it, didn't even ask about the yarn trailing behind me. When she opened the door it sounded just like it sounded half a century ago, like the years meant nothing and had fallen right into the wastepaper basket, with that tinkling bell above the jamb. I went up there and asked the man behind the counter,

Do you all have some lemon drops?

Before he even said anything I knew the answer: they had them sure enough, and when he went to get them for me I stood there awhile and tried to relax a little, for it had been a long walk into Point Blank, and it would be an even longer walk back.

Oly

My life started coming out of the preacher's mouth like scarves from a magic act as he laid there dying in front of us. His breath was so soft the air must have known what it felt like to be touched by a real lover's mouth. I don't know what the others thought because I was waiting for what he was gonna come up with next.

The fact that he was dying didn't bother me all that much, maybe because he kept saying how this was what he'd been waiting for since forever. I haven't ever heard of anybody practicing for his own death before, but I guess you gotta look forward to something. He was wheezing and trying to catch his breath, like sandpaper over knotty pine, the paper saying, *smooth, smooth,* but the wood saying only, *Tough shit.* I thought if anyone could breathe like that at the end of his life and still manage to spit out the words he did then there must be something to it, even as he was talking his way right into the grave.

Something kept busting up inside of me, but I suppose that's a necessary part of coming to the truth. There was hardly anything in my life up till then that I was proud of, not even breaking down game film of the Huskers and coming up with new ways to get the ball to the tight end. The dying preacher made me realize that. Out of the corners of his mouth the whole globe came together to rescue me from myself.

I kept looking at Gus, Y, and Orlando to make out what they were thinking because they'd always been like brothers to me, but I couldn't read their faces. They'd gone graveyard in the eyes. The deathwatch had turned into a poker game, and Y only had eyes for the blind lady. Nobody could ever claim we were witnesses to a rape because none of us were in there and didn't hear a thing except some rustling of bed sheets with a few choking sobs thrown in.

As for me, I was gonna marry the preacher when he died.

I was determined to follow through on it like nothing else in my life.

I'd been lost for so long I knew his marriage proposal might be the last chance I'd ever get to turn my life around, because you know, baby, every other bridge been burned down to the fucking ground. I set them all ablaze myself. I never figured being clean and sober was part of the deal, but that started to change while I watched him die, zeroing in on the grand funk of his mouth and the free style of his hands, which tried to make windmills but couldn't.

Sweetheart was puking up heartache and forgiveness, and

Oly

he made us promise him not to call no doctor no matter what happened, which nobody could do anyway because the blind lady's phone didn't work. She didn't even have locks on the doors or a poodle yapping at her knees. So the preacher's sailboat of death was clear sailing all the way, nothing any of us could do about it short of driving to Point Blank some seven miles away.

But no one was about to do that, no sir.

He wanted to die for us and we weren't gonna get in the way of that twilight development.

My whole life I've been laughing at everything you can shake a stick at, but the grains of my hee-haws were beginning to run out. The girl just sat there at the foot of the bed lapping at the shore of the invisible heat wave coming off him in droves. She didn't look as sad as you might think, was maybe even happy for him. So I'm done trying to make sense out of human behavior, my own or what makes another person tick. I think if you could catch just one good look into somebody's heart you'd weep for what you saw there, the sorrow and the beauty and the thorns growing up around the heartbreak.

I don't know when I started laughing so I couldn't stop.

Maybe you could trace it back to the blind lady's house and the night we broke in. All we did was bust up her place and I laughed about it then, the sound track behind the mayhem and destruction a part of the night that will go down in history as one of the worst of all time.

I'm sorry, blind lady, for what we done to you.

I'll apologize to you sometime in private after the preacher is dead and I marry him like he asked. You're one of the reasons why I live out in the dugout. I moved there because it was free and no one would bother me except for the occasional garter snake or ground squirrel looking for sunflower seeds. A small ravine of old tobacco juice runs like a hairline fracture around my army cot from bygone doubleheaders and the crack of line drives. Some nights the stars are so bright I use them as light bulbs to look at the pussy posse. I've gotten so I know their every look and gesture and hear their high, squeaky voices going madcap on the bedsprings of a cheap motel somewhere. Not a straight man in the world doesn't want naked female company, no matter what he says. And they've never turned me down, not even once. You need people like that sometimes in your corner, especially when you don't have nobody else.

When Gus comes to visit me he don't stay long, not that I can blame him. I have nothin' to offer him except a cup of instant coffee with flavor crystals thrown in like crater dust from the moon. He looks around the dugout with the walls covered with naked women crawling around on all fours. I know he wants to leave as soon as he gets there. I have nothing for him to sit on except a folding chair I found next to a dumpster.

Check out the view, I say, and he looks at the sand hills over the center field fence about 430 feet away. You could get lost in it, like a pilgrim seeking faraway lands. I sweep up the dirt floor before he gets there, my cot just below the lip of the dugout stairs so I can be almost eye-level to the third base line. It's peaceful out there in the dugout, about the most peaceful place there is, even if it gets a little lonely sometimes. You can't hear nothin' but the wind whistling through the fence and crickets hunkered down next to the on-deck circle, but I like it that way. I have a generator cranked up in the back to go over game film and listen to sports radio where everybody's a fucking expert and field-general genius. I even have a board of checkers we sometimes play. I usually beat Gus hands down but I try not to rub it in.

There's something holy about the dugout but I don't know what it is. Maybe it's because it's a few feet below ground, like some kind of shrunken shrine with the echoes of foul balls throw in. People have won and lost in there and made heroes and scapegoats of themselves. Some have sat on my bench with a towel over their heads when they blew a three-run lead, scraping their cleats on the hard cement floor like they're trying to get the taste of defeat out of their mouths. Some even died in head-on collisions driving home from the game. They used to be young and carefree, hitting on pretty girls at late night drive-throughs with mud all over the front of their uniforms from sliding head first into second or third, safe eight times out of ten and a hand up for time-out.

I know how it was. I used to play myself. They'd never be that free again, their whole lives ahead of them but the best part spent right there in the dugout where I live now, five miles from any other dwelling place. Three-two in the bottom of the ninth. Twenty people in the stands but they're all on their feet now with their hands held up to the fence. Digging in at home plate, tap at it with your Easton, once, twice, three times, but never four, the sweet smell of pine tar staying with you to the grave.

It's put up or shut up time—and what are you made of when the game's on the line?

Some nights I cry for no good reason but maybe there is one that goes to the heart of the world. I don't know where the crying comes from, but I always feel clean and pure inside afterward. The sobs are like these piñatas busting out inside of me. I never know where they come from or what they mean, but the wind matches me moan for moan as I blow a stream of snot from one of my nostrils. I don't know if I'm a bad man but I know I'm not a good one. There's a shit of difference if you ask me.

I look at the pussy posse and they're as naked as ever, so naked they look like pigs' throats. It's not even about lust anymore. I wish I could explain it to Gus. Now I just admire their milky white nakedness, the way they smile like hundred-watt light bulbs, how they stretch out on those bear skin rugs in pure female energy pouring over the floor in legs, tits, and ass, with *come hither* written across their slightly open mouths.

He can't say anything to that, and I don't expect him to.

I want people to call me coach, I want my own office and clipboard: I'd like to command the respect of a group of young men devoted to the same blood, sweat, and tears cause. I know I could lead them to the Promised Land. I understand my moral character is suspect, but that doesn't mean I can't distance myself from my addictions and offer some sound instruction on the game.

Some of these kids could get scholarships to D-2 schools if they had me in their corner, maybe even D-1. But all these

noble claims fall on deaf ears. I watch games on my little
ten-incher and I know the plays before they run them, I
know the formations and the sequence of entire drives. I'm
clairvoyant that way. A man deserves a second or third chance,
maybe even a fourth. Don't the bible say something about
that, seven times seventy or some shit like that?

I shoulda known I had no chance the second I was filling
out the application for JV coach at the junior high school.
Home phone number, blank. Home address, blank. List of
references, one, and that was Gus, who's not exactly a pillar of
society. Teaching experience, zip. College degree, nada. Any
degree whatsoever, blankety fucking blank. I was shooting
blanks all over the goddamned place. Only degree I got is
from third-degree burns on my hands.

I sat there in the new Bike gym shorts I'd bought the day
before just for this interview, sporting a brand new crew
cut, and I realized I was fucking kidding myself, that the
secretary looking over at me once in a while and smiling was
just going through the motions, probably trying hard not
to feel sorry for me. There was no way in hell they were ever
gonna hire me as their JV coach, then or ever, and I knew it
for the harsh blinding truth right then and there; the walls
of the office with their shiny certificates and what-not and
the new carpeted floors mocked me for being such a fuck-up
in their tidy world. And me even wearing a whistle around
my neck like it would have made a shit of difference: it was
all a big fucking joke.

'Scuse me a second, Miss—

I said to her, laid the application down on her desk and

walked right out the door and never looked back. Didn't even talk to the head honcho himself. I walked out into the blinding sun, into the dazzling parking lot with all those buffed and waxed cars, stood there like they'd stuck a cattle prod up my ass. I put my dry lips on the whistle I thought would be my most important tool for the molding of young men and blew on it as soft as I could. I stood there blowing on that whistle, hardly making a sound, realizing they'd never take me seriously, let alone give me a chance. I don't know when I'd passed the point of no return, but sure enough it was all over at the ripe old age of thirty-six.

You can't take the dream you got and turn it into what they want: they don't have the eyes to see what you see, to know what you know. It's all just fucking lip service, man, following standard procedures so they won't get slapped with a lawsuit. So I got on my bike and went back to the dugout, where I holed up for a week drinking till I just about faded away and died. If Gus wouldn't have found me and taken me in I don't know if I'd be here today.

That was a few years ago.

I've been getting by ever since, just surviving, you know. Each day's like a wide-awake dream but the promise of a future in coaching ain't a part of it. So the preacher's marriage proposal might be the last chance I have. I know how fucked up it sounds, but I've flat run out of options. When we found him we were still hungover from the night before, trying to get war stories out of Munoz who wouldn't admit a goddamned thing one way or the other. I couldn't understand it because he always used to say all he wanted was to go into the Corps so he could kill some foreign motherfuckers for free and get paid for it.

I believe those were his exact words.

I remembered the time I poured lighter fluid on my hands and lit them on fire, trying to impress them, and how the fire and the pain sealed my sorrow by turning my hands into latex gloves so I'd never touch anything without them on—lobster or mannequin hands they call them down at the bar some Friday nights when things are kinda slow. When you're young and stupid you do crazy shit like that: you do it and you say without saying, *Look at me: you can love me now because I set my hands on fire for you.*

If I could coach I'd tell those young men that no matter what they're going through I've been through it myself. I could speak to them with the voice of authority that's been to hell and back. That's what the powers that be just don't get. They dress real good and say all the right things but they ain't been where I been—they ain't drank long and hard of that bitter cup down to the last nasty dregs. Jesus wasn't the Son of God in the preacher's mouth so much as someone who knew what it was like to be like me, Jared Parker Olson, sniffer of model airplane glue and collector of nasty hardcore porn.

At some down-and-out low point you see the range of your addictions lined up in a row like clay pigeons stretching out to the horizon so far you can't even see the end of them. You see where you went wrong and what it took out of your own stinking hide. I always relied on laughter to get me out of high, tight corners, but this was a different world of whup-ass altogether. What started out as so damn funny became a weeping fit of hysteria about to flood out all over the blind lady's floor.

For the tears and waste of it, for the crying shame.

I'd clean up my act, avoid the temptation of paint thinner and aftershave. Throw all my nasty clothes into a trash bin and set them on fire, Adios muchachos. Maybe the good looks of my youth would come back to me like rubbing the sweet spot of a genie's bottle. Nobody ever called me a lamb before, but the funny thing was, it fit like a glove.

You gave me that, preacher baby, you told me how it was. Everything else is just so much bullshit to wade through, war stories and bar fights, swapping cock sizes out on the playground. After you die I'm pedaling back as fast as I can to change and start my life all over for what you gave me, away from Point Blank where everyone is dying, the least populated county in the Lower 48. The blind lady can have all the open space she wants.

Then I reminded myself of something I thought I had forgotten. Remember the time Big Shot Ross let you detail his '67 candy apple red 'Stang for forty dollars and you did it with tender pride, caressing that sweet-ass bitch down to the wheel rims like nobody ever would again. You used cotton swabs on the dash with loving care like you were painting a young thing's toenails and hard-to-reach places around the steering column, and you were into it, man, so totally dedicated to making that beautiful baby shine and shine beyond the forty dollars or any other pocket change the rich s.o.b. threw at you. Because it wasn't about the money then, but something else nobody could ever buy. He was sitting in his ranch-style house that seemed to sprawl on for acres, pretending to read the newspaper but watching all the while. But it didn't matter as you made love to that car, whispering in her ears, *Oly's here for you, baby, ain't no one ever gonna love you like this again. Remember that when I'm gone.*

You made a vow to that car and you made good on it, even if you only had two precious hours with her and fat-ass eagle eyes hawking your every move as if you'd tried to steal something out of her, which you never would have done. You'd rather die than take advantage of her like that. It was like being in a church on holy rollin' Firestones.

See, that's the thing you couldn't tell Ross or anybody else, what you couldn't make them understand: you would have done her for free, just for the chance of waxing her sides. Because that's all that mattered. For the sheer privilege of being around a classic automobile like that.

You were a pro with her with no bad intent and maybe you can get that feeling back, Oly, breathe on it like a candle flame cupped in your bare burned-up hands to take care of again. Preacher's opened the door a crack, a little seam of daylight for the first time in years. You already had that loving know-how down cold, nobody had to teach you about it, nobody could take it away. You just had it. And maybe it's come back again in the preacher's mouth, just maybe. So blow the dust off, Oly, get ready to use it again. Because, goddammit, you hopeless sonofabitch, here it comes one last time and don't you ever fucking forget it.

Gus

Oly's trying not to laugh, but I don't know what's so funny: he's always cracking up over the damndest things. Now it smells like something sweet and holy in the room, but it's hard to make out what it is: hemp, weed, or sandalwood drying in the sun.

The girl's sitting at the foot of the bed and has hardly moved at all. She's not freaked out like you might think. You can see the preacher's gnarled veins on his hands, like a map of some country in South America way up in the Andes. Miss Marian just sits in the corner like she's seen it all before, though she can't even see, the moons of her dead white eyes going down all over again. I feel bad for her, on top of the guilt I already have that I've been hauling around for years. No one ever officially apologized to her that I know of and here we are again, bringing in a near-dead preacher shouting Jesus and the end of the world with the girl following behind with a wagonload of bibles.

I don't know what his purpose is in telling people his sob story, but he's gotta have one. I'm not religious, unless you take worshipping the Huskers for religion. The girl cries a little, then stops, resting her head against his feet, not making any sound, her pretty head shaking up and down then growing still. Nobody says a word. What can we say? We didn't even know the dude. All the passion and hysterics rise and fall with the preacher and it's quiet now, hush-hush except for the rain and lightning that comes to take snapshots of the room.

So what the hell are all the fireworks for?

Why has he been shouting like that ever since we found him?

I saw my grandpa and uncle right before they died, but it was nothing like this. Grandpa Wayne was unconscious and Uncle Ben had a smile plastered on his face for four days straight. I think he died as drunk as he'd been for the last twelve years of his life. The preacher's in a different category altogether, way off the charts about whatever he's ranting about, raving something fierce and pleading his cause like he's two or three people and none of them agree. It's tough to make fun of him, though, dead or alive. The rest of us are just standing here, not knowing what to do or say. We've done everything we could. He won't let us call a doctor. It's like this unspoken bond between us, we want to play it out and see what happens to the preacher after it's all said and done. For some reason I miss him already and I don't even know why.

But it's goddamned nerve-wracking just standing here,

Yarborough, Munoz, Oly, and me, plus the girl and Miss Marian, like we're waiting for the roof to cave in. Miss Marian knows who you are without seeing you, like she can I.D. your footsteps. She's spooky that way. Even a sigh can give you away. It's better not to breathe around her or she'll know it's you. I've never felt right around her after what we did to her place—but nobody ever really has felt comfortable around her as far as I can tell.

That's always been a part of her reputation, whether she deserves it or not. She gives off this aura of mind reading or clairvoyance, condemning you without condemning you just by letting you be your own naked self. There's no sense to it as far as I can see. A hundred times I've wanted to apologize to her, and I almost did a handful of times. But I just couldn't follow through with it. I've been hanging on the edge of confession so long I don't hardly know what I'd do without it. Maybe I'm afraid she wouldn't accept it, or she'll start telling me how bad that night was for her. I don't know if I could handle that. But she keeps showing up in my dreams, sitting there like she is now, watching me with those dead white eyes, her gnarled fingers holding an onion or a ball of yarn with two crows next to her on either side, their wings open wide along with their clawing beaks.

I mow her yard and run errands for her: I even got a bat out of this same room once. But I can't tell her I was one of them that night. So what the hell can you do with that? She knows I was there anyway. She even knows what kinds of tattoos I have, and nobody told her about them. Why the hell would they? How can she describe what she's never seen before—how can she know what they look like if she can't see and I've never been around her with my shirt off? The other guys, they enjoyed what we did, even Munoz, who just got back from defusing bombs in Iraq.

But I didn't. I only did it because I didn't want to look like a pussy in front of them, which I know is a lame fucking excuse, but what can I do about it now? Tell it to a sixteen-year-old. That's how old I was. We broke into her place while she was sitting right about where she is now. We took a cuckoo clock, thirty bucks cash, some figurines, a painting off the wall, and a fire extinguisher. That was it. But it was still way too much. And here we all are again, standing at the scene of the crime where we never got caught, older now and each one of us spiraling out of control in his own way, standing in Miss Marian's place that we trashed years ago because we knew she lived alone.

It's the lowest thing I've ever done, breaking into a blind woman's place and going through her personal stuff while she sits there in front of us, telling us again and again in a quiet but shaky voice, *You don't have to do this*. Doesn't matter that I drank a bottle of Everclear and half a bottle of vodka. Doesn't matter that she knew who we were and still didn't press charges. It was wrong and I see that now. Why couldn't I see it before? Nothing I do can make up for it or erase the picture from my mind of her sitting there no bigger than a vacuum bag. I know Oly feels the same way. He said so once. That's why I try to watch out for her now, because I know how vulnerable she is way out here by herself.

I don't know about Y and Orlando, we've never talked

about it. All of us should have gotten the hell out of Point Blank when we had the chance. But I guess we really didn't have much opportunity, except for Munoz when he joined the Marines. It's not like we were Ivy League material or anything. But maybe we just didn't give ourselves a fighting chance. It messes with your mind just thinking about it sometimes, wondering if you missed a train deep in the middle of the night that was meant just for you, and once it's gone there's just no getting on it. Now Y just got out of prison and Oly lives by himself in a dugout at the edge of town, which is hard to even wrap my mind around, and Munoz has come back from Iraq quieter than I've ever seen him, not saying a word about his time over there.

And what do I do?

I take care of Aunt Tish and keep an eye on Miss Marian after losing my job at Plains Power Tools.

I don't know why we're still standing here, stinking up the place like gutted fish. We didn't catch jack shit before we saw the preacher waving his hands and hollering on the road, then collapsing in a heap. We stayed up all night the night before, trying to get war stories out of Orlando. Of course we drank too much. Now it looks like the girl is about to do his toenails. One of my tattoos is an oriental dragon and it covers my back in blue indigo ink smooth as silk with fire roaring out of its mouth. I got it in Lincoln eight summers ago on O Street. I need two mirrors to see it. Miss Marian described it to me once out of nowhere, telling me what it looked like. The way she talked about it made me think it had been on her mind for awhile.

Danny, why did you put that dragon on your back?

I didn't know what to say. I made something up and changed the subject pronto.

Preacher says the light will come down and draw all of us up into it and there's no way to escape it. Then he's off on another tangent like some state patrol scanner after midnight, sometimes coming in loud and clear and other times giving off nothing but static and shrieking amens. Right now I'm trying not to check out the girl's ass but it's kinda hard. She's bending over in front of us and it's tight against her white dress. I guess old habits die hard. I think of the lyrics from a song I heard long ago, *Look away, Look away,* but I'm not even sure these are the right words. She can't be more than thirteen or fourteen, but she's already good-looking. Anyone can see that. Seems like every pretty girl in Point Blank goes away or loses her looks at an early age.

When I lost my job at Plains I got drunk for two weeks and slept with anyone who'd go home with me after last call at Dubber's. I fell asleep most nights in the flatbed of my pickup. The future rang up a bunch of zeroes and I sailed through each one without even clipping the sides. I saw my dragon tattoo in a cheap motel room mirror while I was fucking this fat chick from Valentine. I don't even remember her name. I think it was Dawn or Donna. We both shook and wobbled on the rickety bed like bowls of clear-colored Jell-O. After we were done she told me she'd been raped as a little girl. I didn't know what to say, or what to do or think. She gave me this personal information and all I could do was lay there and feel bad about it, along with so many other things, it's like they were crowding out the rest of me to leave nothing behind but blank.

When will the day come when I can take my shame and bury it for good? When will I feel like there's something important I have to do? I don't have any marketable skills except hunting birds. I lead parties of businessmen sometimes in the fall for pheasant and quail. Money's pretty good, but it's mostly seasonal work. Maybe I'll take hunting expeditions to Alaska. But I need to get my GED. I thought high school was pretty much bullshit and still do, so it's like they have you by the balls either way. I thought I'd have some land by now and could farm it full time but that turned out to be a pipe dream. People around here can only afford to farm part time if they farm at all. I call it Farmer's Mouth: they talk the talk and wear all the Capehart gear but they don't have the resources or the know-how to back it up, including me. So what the hell is it good for?

A hundred some years ago my great-great-grandfather fought the Indians a few miles from here. He took an arrow in the shoulder. Aunt Tish keeps the arrowhead in a glass container in her drawer that she takes out on special occasions, like Christmas or when Uncle Louie gets drunk and starts yelling, *Bring out the arrowhead! Bring out the arrowhead for Danny!* The arrowhead is dark and made of chipped flint, but it doesn't look sharp enough to do much damage. I suppose it could still kill you dead enough if it was shot in the right place. My great-great-grandfather lost sixty percent of his blood but still managed to fight off five of them with his Spencer rifle in a sod house they shot full of flaming arrows before the cavalry arrived. I used to sneak in as a kid and touch the arrowhead for good luck, sometimes poking it into my shoulder hard enough to draw blood.

I needed to bleed somehow. Still do. It's important to feel what it felt like, even if it's just a pale reflection of the real thing. Maybe that's why we were so keen in getting war stories out of Munoz. Sometimes I'm in there with my great-great-grandpa in my mind as we fight them off and wipe the sweat from our eyes. Then you can imagine in a tiny way what it used to mean to be a man. To this day I'm amazed the Indians would try to fight us with bows and arrows. Seems like certain suicide to me. But you have to admire them for it in a way, though I've never said this to Aunt Tish. Might seem like I was taking their side after we won it all.

The tattoos on my body tell a story and all of them added up together have something to say about going through life on a mythical journey. That's what a girl told me once when we were naked in bed, because my whole body is covered in them. The only place left on me that doesn't have a tattoo is my face and a space below my heart. Everything else is high-def panorama, things you see in nightmares and dreams that disappear when you open your eyes, only here they're on me in black and indigo blue and star-spangled red. I didn't know I was collecting them to tell a story, but she kept insisting I was. After she said it something clicked in my mind, like it had been waiting for me since I was a kid.

Sometimes I drive down country roads with Oly and we have a case of Bud in the back. Oly brings along his .30-.30. We don't hardly say a word because there's no need to. Everything

we could have said has been said already by better men than
us. He shoots out the window while I'm doing sixty. If he's
drunk enough he'll shoot at goddamned anything. It doesn't
have to be alive or dead or hardly moving, it doesn't even
have to be a target. The sky will do if there's nothing else,
the one that presses down on all of us out here. One time
he even shot at a row of corn just as a general direction. He
seems sad and heart-broke when he's doing it, like he's lost
or about to cry or throw himself out of the truck. I don't
even think he wants to shoot most of the time, but what the
hell's a rifle for outside of deer and antelope season? I play
Metallica and Oly will shoot out the window at anything he
sees that gets in the way between him and the sadness that's
gnawing away at his insides.

One time I asked him what he was shooting at and he said
something I'll never forget: He said,

I'm shooting the ghost of Tom Osborne.

But Oly, I told him, Osborne's still alive.

Didn't make any sense because Oly worships the ground
Osborne walks on. He thinks Osborne's Christ walking on
water. The greatest college football coach who ever lived, and
Oly thinks he needs to shoot his ghost wherever he sees him,
Ol' Tom standing there like a statue on the sidelines with
those long red slacks in a broken-down barn door or railroad
crossing sign, even a boarded-up hardware store rusting
with used Pennzoil cans. That's how fucked-up things have
become. Osborne retires and goes to Washington in politics
and the whole program goes straight to hell, along with
everyone in Point Blank who were there already but didn't

know it till the Huskers went south. Then this preacher comes along and starts saying all the things we already knew deep in our bones but didn't have the words for, all the things so dead-on and true, like each one of us was blown out of the cannon of our mouths to be swallowed up in his.

Who else could talk the way he does, spelling it out in such vivid forms it's like they're white-hot crosses branded into your forehead? I smelled my own burning skin once when I got a tattoo of a mako shark on my right quad, and it was kinda like that: instead of getting sick I was almost glad that it was finally happening to me, that I was turning into some other kind of dude that I'd never been before. That's as close as I can get to explaining it, like this town that isn't really even a town. We call it Point Blank because there's nowhere to hide and nothing to protect you, just sky all around and land rolling out in every direction. I've been away just once, for two months when I went to Missouri to help out my cousin Neal, and I felt something was missing even then.

You know what I think was missing? Nothing, that's what. And the funny thing about nothing is you can't replace it with anything else: it's either real nothing or it's not nothing at all. I wish I could talk to the preacher about this and a few other things besides. I'd ask him some questions and listen real hard for the answers. But I'm afraid to in front of the others.

I'd say, *Preacher, I'm honored to have you die here at our hands and tell us these important things about your sinful life and the overall sins of men and how we forget about doing good in the process of claiming our share and all those other bad things we do and keep on doing because it feels good and leads to despair. I gotcha there, Preacher. And Preacher, someone could have loved me from an appleseed like you said and kept right on going but I'm no tree, just myself and what am I supposed to do about the disappointment of being who I am and Miss Marian and all the other things I done that I ain't proud of?* It's my goal to put the preacher on me, to get a picture of him tattooed on my body. Other guys have more tattoos than me but theirs don't tell a story like mine do—a story of violence and a story of waste, a story of not knowing where to turn before the light turns green and you're all alone. It's the whole story of America and the good life in Nebraska, and I carry it around on my redneck skin. Old-timers say I'm still young, but they don't know: they think the world is the same as when they were growing up but it isn't anymore, and there's not a damn thing you can do about it.

I have 140 tattoos on my body all told, and I wish I had more skin to somehow say the things I want to scream and describe. I wasn't born to be a loser but it seems like losing is all I can manage around here, in the air, the dust kicking up from the road, the ConAgra corn, Schmitty the town drunk, Janice Schultz the town whore, Miss Marian the town mystery. We all have a part to play, and I suppose we'll play it till we die. I'm not feeling sorry for myself, it's just the godforsaken truth. Now the girl stands up and stretches a little. She's smoothing her dress that was so recently a veil of tears. Then holy fucking Christ, she does the last thing in the world you'd think anyone would do right then: she tries out a few dance steps as the preacher moans and groans and slobbers, cranking up for another one of his speeches.

Mady

One night I found one thousand dollars in a bowling bag sitting in a ditch a mile away from a Super 8 outside of Lincoln, Nebraska, tens and twenties wrapped up in thick rubber bands. The bag had a broken zipper on it but no bowling ball because it was so stuffed with money. It was the kind of bag you could see someone carrying strange stuff in, handcuffs or jewels, a brick of pure gold, maybe even some poor sucker's head. I fanned the cash through my fingers just like you see in the movies: it made the sound of a boat way out in the Everglades.

I'd found money before on the sidewalk or next to a stop sign, but nothing like this. This cash was new, with hardly a crease in it, all those old-fashioned presidents as young as they'd ever be in the hands of a few shady characters. I'd wandered pretty far from the hotel, though I could see it off the highway like a yellow life raft way out in the ocean. I'd seen so many hotels and motels just like it, though each one had its own bleeding voice crying so low only a howling dog could hear it. The bowling ball that should have been in there was rolling in a gutter somewhere with a big fat guy behind it cussing up a storm in his red clown shoes. Mr. Gene had started practicing his deathbed a half hour before and I was out walking around ten o'clock, which is kinda late when you're in a new place and don't know your way around. I told him I'd be down in the lobby people-watching but no one was there but the lady behind the counter with a phone glued to her ear, laughing and blushing and not paying attention to anything going on around her.

So I walked out of the hotel.

I did that sometimes when we were traveling. Mr. Gene had his routines and I had mine. Sometimes that meant walking around by myself, going no place in particular but just going. I had on my jeans jacket and brand new tennis shoes so I figured I could handle a few drops of rain. The idea just popped into my head. I was sitting there on the lobby couch next to a plastic palm tree, and I was kinda restless. I didn't set out to deceive Mr. Gene. I just figured I'd walk around for awhile outside even though it was cold and windy, get some fresh air and smoke a few before coming in on the end of his deathbed practice that always involved a lot of moaning and some prayers that didn't make much sense. How he could practice his deathbed without falling asleep I never could figure out. A few cars and trucks passed me along the way, one of them even slowing down like the driver was about to ask me to get in. I saw his glowing brake lights like two dragon eyes about fifty feet away. But I wasn't scared. I had my guardian angel, Rufus, with me, who used to be an old black man with rickety knees. Rufus floated around the edge of danger, his wings tied together with guitar strings he used to pick at when he was alive. I just changed direction and started walking out into the field and the driver stayed there for a little while before he pulled away.

Then I saw some bright pieces of green paper fluttering up into the air in a barren cornfield before they were sucked away by the wind. Right away I knew it was money, one of those things you just know. I figured if there was any more it had to be close by, so I went a little farther out where the cash had come from, thinking I could surprise Mr. Gene by buying him a Chinese dinner. He was always partial to egg rolls and a little pot of green tea. So I just kept on walking over the uneven ground, getting my shoes all muddy, but I didn't care too much. Mr. Gene didn't notice things like that anyway. It was a lot farther out in the field than I expected but then suddenly I stumbled across the bag, like a hole punched in the darkness. I stood over it a long time, my pulse pounding hard against my temples. It's not that I was afraid to pick it up, only that I knew what was in there was probably wanted by a lot of people who were willing to do some pretty strong stuff to get it.

I imagined the guy who left it as if I'd seen him in my dreams, with a handlebar mustache and three-day beard, bloodshot eyes and shaky hands that had been putting up drywall before turning to a life of crime. I called him Jake. And Jake was in a serious world of hurt. You could feel his desperation out in that field and somewhere else besides, the way a single crumb clung to his mustache like it was the only bright spot left in his Wonder Bread life. I smelled the stale corn chips of his fear, the money he smuggled so carefully so he could come all the way out here and throw it all away. Jake could have fled the scene of the crime or before the deal was done—but something had gone wrong and he had made a run for it before they could catch him. I felt sorry for Jake, like the money he forgot or lost was an only child who had slipped through his fingers and drowned. He could have been the father I never knew or some other long lost uncle I didn't know I had, spending his days and nights within a couple of feet of a case of beer.

Some headlights swung across my back, sweeping across the land before they faded in the distance. I should have worn some kind of camouflage outfit but I was so far out there I figured no one could see me unless they really squinted. With my jeans jacket and all, you couldn't hardly see me except below the knees. The sky was lit up from the traffic on the highway and the lights from the city; I felt like I was standing in some kind of huge dark room without any doors. I looked back at the Super 8, then I opened the bag and counted all the money, holding up the bills to what little light there was.

I could hear litter ringing all around me like tiny Christmas bells that rang faster then slower then speeded up again—strange echoes from a thousand broken wrecking balls. For a second I thought about keeping the bag and just walking away. I thought about it—not because I didn't love

Mr. Gene but because I wondered what it would be like to be on my own. I knew that day was coming. But the truth was Mr. Gene needed me like you need a shoehorn or a windbreaker, something that could help him in a pinch but not something he ever thought too much about one way or the other until he really had to. This didn't make me angry or sad, it's just the way it was. He was mine to take care of somehow, even though I was the kid and he was the grown-up and he had kidnapped me and had somebody set the house on fire, Mama's face like a smiling picture I had to concentrate on real hard to remember. That's just how it was. How you end up taking responsibility for someone else can be downright strange and mysterious, no matter how old you are or where you come from or what you think you should do.

I knew all along that Mr. Gene's caterpillar lips would be with me wherever I went, shaping words and sounds hardly nobody ever could make heads or tails of that would turn into butterflies one day. I always believed that, strange, bright butterflies flying the world over in crazy loop-de-loops that would save somebody from going under. So of course I was going back to the Super 8, though holding the bag of money made me feel a helluva lot bigger than I was, towering almost, the size of a small house getting bigger all the time, like before too long everyone would be able to see me and x-ray my soul and call in the National Guard because I was crushing cars underfoot, like Godzilla.

There was more money in that bag than I'd ever seen in my life—and whether it was Jake's or somebody else's, I was holding it so I knew I had to do something with it. I started walking back to the Super 8 and whistling to give myself courage because I didn't know if Jake had dropped the money in the last twenty-four hours or not or if someone wasn't even then searching the highway for it. Sometimes it's a really good thing to be a girl like me, to not have to worry about intimidating people by the way you look. I held the bag close to my side like a purse and you couldn't probably even tell the difference. But the Super 8 seemed far away—and then snow started mixing with sleet and I started to run like someone was after me.

Because maybe someone was. Maybe someone was watching the field and had Jake tied up in the back seat with a razor blade held at his throat. The faster I ran the more I thought someone was watching me, ready to follow me into the lobby and up to the room where Mr. Gene was laid out on his deathbed, murmuring faint words of praise. Then they'd probably shoot us and cut us up in the bathtub into bite-size pieces. It was possible, maybe even likely. So before I got to the bright lights of the highway and the parking lot of the Super 8 I laid down in the field and watched the traffic for awhile with the bowling bag under me, trying to catch my breath and get my bearings. The Super 8 looked so peaceful and downright mellow, like it was about to melt into a puddle of buttermilk. I wanted to make sure the coast was clear because one thousand dollars was a lot of money and even Jake might want to hunt me down for it. There were only five cars in the parking lot with just a few lights on in the rooms, like the broken teeth of a hockey player.

Mady, you can do this, I said. But maybe it was just Rufus putting the words into my head, because I don't usually talk that way. After a few minutes I stood up and smoothed out my jeans jacket and skirt, which by then were a little muddy. I took three deep breaths and could see them scroll into the air like exhaust from a tailpipe. I wouldn't go into the lobby. I had my room key and I'd go in some other entrance. So I started walking toward the hotel, trying not to hurry but also trying to get there as fast as I could, keeping my head down. Only two cars passed me along the way. I went to the back entrance of the building and then flew up the stairs, running two or three at a time. When I reached the second floor I stopped and looked down the hallway. Empty. Not a sound, except for someone's TV laughing out loud.

I looked at the bag in my hand. Anyone who saw me would wonder what was in it. Because it sure didn't look like I was ready to bowl. So I ran back down the stairs again and ducked into the ice room to figure out what to do next. I heard the ice machine humming and a few new cubes falling into place, one tinkling avalanche at a time. Someone was bound to come in for ice before too long, and there I was, standing there with a thousand bucks. I rummaged through the trash container and found a Burger King bag, so I put all the money in the Burger King bag and stuffed the bowling bag down into the trash. I didn't figure a little ketchup would hurt the cash, maybe even give it some flavor. Whoever went to BK must have had quite a few whoppers because all the money fit, but just barely. And I started to breathe a little easier, even managed a chuckle or two. I was free and clear. If anyone saw me they'd think I was just some smart-aleck kid bringing back burgers for her dad. In fact, the old switcharoo made me tingle all over and gave me a shiver up my spine for what could have happened. But I felt okay—maybe even a little proud for thinking on my feet.

I walked out of the ice room with my head held high, almost daring someone to stop me and ask me what was in the bag. I'd sneer at them, I'd laugh, I'd draw it out to the bitter end, saying, *What does it look like, dude? Whoppers.* And then I'd just walk away without looking back, not even so much as a glance. And I have to admit, it felt good having all that money in the palm of my hand, swinging free and easy at the end of it. I'd probably never see money like that again in my life; the most I'd ever seen up till then was four twenties on top of each other. I knew what I had to do with it, but that didn't mean I couldn't strut around with it for awhile, trying out what it felt like to be rich, knowing I could walk into the lobby and say, without blinking, *We'd like a room for the next ten nights,* just to see how that clerk looked at me. The money made me feel confident and strong, big enough to bet on ball games. So I walked around the hotel with money in a Burger King bag, up and down the hallways of the first and second floors, feeling all that green stoke up my gumption for the sheer hell of it.

Mr. Gene, I'd say, *how 'bout we knock off this bible business for awhile and stay someplace where they have an indoor pool?* I wish I could have seen his face on that one. Because I was just me, Mady Kim Seymore, but I was rich—rich in a way no other girl I ever heard tell of was, rich for a time in the

Super 8 while Mr. Gene was on his back, going through his last rites like they had the taste of cinnamon in them. But it's funny about money, you know, how the high of having it wears off so soon to test your nerves, like a sugar high or some other artificial flavor, how the longer you hold onto it the more it plays with your mind. When I just had a dollar I felt free and open to everything—but when I had a thousand I almost got a headache trying to think of ways to spend it. And none of them seemed right somehow, just a little off, fur coats and diamond rings, maybe some new Nikes. Don't get me wrong, I was glad to tote it, but something was missing.

Then on about my seventh lap on the second floor I heard somebody crying in a room: it was a lady's voice, in room 201. She was sobbing, bawling her eyes out. I stood there for awhile, still as a statue, trying to make out who she was talking to though I know eavesdropping isn't very nice. I snuck up to her room and pressed my head against the door. She was talking to someone on the phone and whoever it was was making her miserable. The TV was on in the background, talking about this year's fashion or the next. *Don't. Jerry. Please. We don't have to. Jerry. Don't. Please. Don't say that. Jerry. Please. Don't say that.* I couldn't stop listening to her broken words that never finished what they were trying to say. She was rocking back and forth on the bed, I could see it in my mind, talking to that jerk named Jerry. This went on for a long time, the woman crying and pleading in there and me standing next to her door with my ear pressed up against it.

What could you do about that?

What could you say?

I looked at the money in my hand, the money that people wanted so bad. When I was all grown up and on my own, I'd have to open a bank account and fill out all these papers, get a plastic card and password I couldn't forget, pay bills, buy groceries, get Christmas presents for friends. I'd have to carry cash in my purse for emergencies, take it out after a meal, leave a tip, pay a cab driver, deposit quarters in a Laundromat washing machine, hand some twenties to someone standing behind a ticket booth at a rock concert, watch the money disappear, leaves of green going up in smoke, disappearing, fading away, whether I bought spoons at Wal*Mart or some other place, on and on and on it would go until the day I died.

Jerry. It doesn't have to be this way. Please. I'll get it somehow. Jerry. Jerry. Jerry? The sonofabitch hung up on her. I heard her put the phone back on its cradle. It was just me and her on the whole second floor on a cold rainy night turning to snow outside Lincoln, the woman in her room all by herself and Mr. Gene on the floor above, moving into his own private Twilight Zone. And you know how some people cry, how when they weep it does something strange to you like an out-of-body experience, hearing their sadness in sounds just like themselves but also far away, remote, like nothing on earth could touch or reach them. *It doesn't have to be this way,* she said. And she was right; she was dead-on. Whatever way it was wasn't the way it should have been—because Jerry didn't know I was listening.

Maybe that's what they mean when they say life isn't fair. Maybe that's why you hear about people hanging themselves in hotel rooms like 201, or overdosing on sleeping pills and vodka or whatever they can get their hands on. All the things you hear about and all the things you call by some kind of name, a Super 8 that really isn't so super, just another hotel outside a city on the plains where you can get free muffins in the morning between seven and ten, even if they're a little hard. And just a few cars in the parking lot, one of them beat up and rusting, the clerk downstairs talking to her boyfriend with dreams of flying away to Cancun or anywhere but where she was, Mr. Gene on the final lap of his deathbed, trying to squeeze the most out of preparing for something that's hard to prepare for—and Jake on the run, his heart about to jump through his chest, a revolver in the glove compartment and a pack of smokes in the passenger seat where someone should have been, listening to his story. None of it seemed very fair at all. I put my free hand up on the door and drew it down, trying to touch her through the wood that probably wasn't even wood but some kind of new fangled material. She needed to know someone had heard her. She needed to realize someone understood without knowing exactly what was going on.

I went down to the lobby and went up to the counter where the girl stood there on the phone. *I need to borrow a pen*, I said, and without missing a beat she pushed a pen to me on the counter and went back to talking to Mr. Sunshine.

Dear 201

I wrote on the Burger King Bag

This cash is for you. Don't turn it in because somebody else will try to claim it. Take it, it's yours. Tell that jackass Jerry he can stick it where the sun don't shine. Well, you don't have to say that but that's what I would tell him.

Yours truly,
A Stranger

I walked back up to her room and put my ear against her door: 201 was crying and sniffling, probably wrapping the sheets around herself. I put the bag down at the foot of the door, knocked as hard as I could three times, then took off at a dead sprint down the hallway, running as fast as I could.

No way could she have seen me. I can get up to a flat-out sprint in no time at all and I hardly made a sound on the soft carpet of the hallway. I hope she didn't give all of it to that jackass Jerry. When I got back to Mr. Gene he was just in the last of his death throes, nothing major I hadn't seen before but maybe a little more drawn out than usual. I thought he might ask me where I'd been, but he was off doing tours of the moon, where he'd already died a hundred times. *I'm going to take a shower*, I said, and if he heard me I didn't notice because, for some reason I still don't understand, I started crying to myself after I shut the door behind me and turned on the water full blast.

Yarborough

Heavyweight champ of all time cruising up to me in knee-deep water, rainbows breaking out all across your spine. Biggest, sweetest fish I ever saw. Somehow the dying preacher made me think of you.

I'm five years old standing in the lake and Mama's still alive and I don't even have a rod in my hands, watching you come into the shallows, blazing a trail of glory from a hundred yards away, nosing in low and steady a few inches above your shadow, sleek as a torpedo.

How many of you been baptized in desire?

the preacher asks, but none of us know what to say, so nobody says anything. I could have picked that fish up with my own two hands, could have lifted it out of the shining water above my head like dripping stained-glass windows with the sun coming off in sparkling dew. But I was too young to know this was a once-in-a-lifetime thing, too blown away by the fish that keeps coming back to me when I least expect it.

Mama's talking on the deck, but she's not talking to me: she's laughing and talking to Grandmama and it's more just like a tone. But that's okay—least I can hear her and that's the important thing. She's laughing, and then before I know it she's gone, so that's all I ever remember, the soft tinkling piano keys of her laughter at the end of summer.

But my God, what a fish that was. I've never seen anything like it. The preacher's coughing and wheezing like a sprained accordion babbling out some incoherence nobody can make sense of, so I just keep my eyes fixed on the blind lady, like she's the magnet and I'm the iron filings. She's as rock steady as they come and I know that from personal experience. We have a secret between us going on almost twenty years now. I've told her about the fish in my mind, but it's like she already knew: she's seen it all before in some other place.

It's like this, Miss Marian: I could have caught the fish with my hands but I didn't want to catch it. I let it touch me because any other way would have ruined it somehow. I know that now. You gotta admit that's some kind of fish that would come up and do that, so the usual rules don't apply. You watch the fish come up to you, you feel it bump against your shin, it swims away and that's the whole story. But what it felt like, there's just no end to it because it keeps going on forever.

Miss Marian would listen as I told her about it. Maybe that's even why I wanted to break into her house, everything else just a setup for the quiet listening of her hands in a room off by ourselves, after taking off my clothes and touching her while she laid there stiff as a shoebox lid before what happened happened in the pitch black darkness of her bedroom.

And Mama's laughing up on the deck in her carefree way, lighter than helium in a carnival balloon. The old man's long gone, lost to the rumors of drop-dead drunk. I never liked the sonofabitch anyway. I didn't figure on following in his footsteps, but like they say, it's in the blood. Can hardly even remember what he looked like, except for the redness of his eyes after a hard night of drinking. He died sometime later on, outside a roadhouse near Oklahoma City, stabbed in the neck then bleeding to death, checking his hand once or twice like he was checking on the time.

We could have gone a long way like that, Mama and me, up there with grandmamma, but we didn't know our time was almost up. I want to hear her hum again so bad I can almost hear it, not for my own sake, but for hers.

I promised Mama at her grave I'd try to make good but I couldn't hold my end up on it. So I never made another promise again. I swore when I went to prison I'd die before I became somebody's bitch, but one day that changed, too, and there was nothing I could do about it. I thought I had proved myself by kicking the righteous shit out of one of them three days before. But payback comes in droves.

I was pushing a laundry bin down a hallway and they jumped me. I never saw them coming. You almost have to admire how they planned it in a way from a stone-cold perspective: not a one of them could take me down alone.

While it was happening the blind lady rose up before me, her face glowing like a halo as they tore my asshole to shreds.

I kept seeing her, glowing brighter all the time until I could just barely make out her face smiling down on me. I couldn't believe she could do that after what we did to her, shine down on me like that while they took turns. Her face was like this bright shining stone that's soft at the edges, and then I knew or understood something I never knew before, but it was a long time before I could make any sense out of it.

Up until they jumped me I saw the world as one long string of survival mode, with a few kicks thrown in to make it all worthwhile. I just plain didn't give a fuck after Mama died. I was ten years old, bounced from home to home, ending up in Point Blank with my step-uncle. He did the best he could but there's not much you can do when you hate each other's guts. I always had a problem with someone telling me what to do, especially if that particular someone was an asshole. I wasn't looking for advice or mercy or leniency anyway. But I saw the blind lady; she was fixed in my mind like the sun and I didn't want that picture to ever leave me and I don't think it ever will.

There's goodness in this world despite the evil shit that happens and you just have to believe it. Because why else would she appear to me that way?

I never told this before. I won't tell it again.

You hear me?

A hundred times in prison I started to write her, but each time I never could follow through with it. Instead I wrote the letters in my head, telling her how it was and what I come to think about what we did and our time spent in the bedroom together, stretched out in the dark.

In the dream letter of my mind I say

Dear Miss Marian—
What we did to you in your house is something I can't stop
thinking about. I'm here in prison for armed robbery and I
want you to know I been thinking of you, not in a bad way
like you might think after what happened but in a good way.
So this is what I been thinking.

If I ever get out of here in one piece I'd like to talk to you about
it—how you forgave us for what we did by never reporting us
to the police and how this is a mystery to me nobody can ever
solve but you. I'd be grateful if you could tell me sometime how
you came to forgive us for what we done, though I know I don't
deserve an explanation.

I never thought you were afraid in that room, except for a
little trembling in your voice. I could tell you didn't hate us for
what we did and that's another one of the things I don't under-
stand—how you could keep from hating us for what we did to
you. We deserved to be hated. We deserved to be feared. In here
I am hated and I hate back all the time, but then there's this
little growing part of me that can't hate anymore and I think
you planted that in me that night and it's been growing ever
since. It don't mean I still don't want revenge. It only means
that it's there and it keeps coming back and I don't know what
to make of it.

You gave me something that night that I can't stop think-
ing about. I never got along with any teacher in my life but if
I had, I think it would be something like that, like this lesson
you gave that can't be found in any book.

I'm sorry about what I done. I see how bad it is now. I'm ashamed I touched you that way. I wish that was the crime I'm paying for and not this one, but I suppose it all comes to the same thing sooner or later, and getting caught at something else doesn't mean you won't pay for the other stuff you did. That's the way it's gotta be.

The letter goes on, filling up twenty notebooks. Mama's on the deck, laughing in her easy chair. I see the concrete floor with the grainy specks in it, not while it's happening but later on, night after night and during the day when it keeps flashing into my mind. Hogs are better than people and I always figured myself to be one of the hogs but I must not be. I have this faint trail of decency in me petering out in the woods somewhere and it almost makes me wanna cry, but I don't have any tears and I can't cry them anyway, so what the hell are they good for? Wanting to cry has to be good enough because that's all I got left. I don't have to spell it out for Miss Marian. She the only one I ever cried in front of, even after Mama died.

I was out just three months when I saw one of them at a bar in North Platte, looking a little forlorn and nursing a beer, probably because he wasn't with his ass-riding buddies. I saw him but he didn't see me. He was sitting up at the bar with empty stools on each side of him, leaning on his elbows with Stevie Ray Vaughn blaring out of the jukebox. I'm sitting back at a booth with some woman I met two hours before and I see his face in the mirror above the glowing bottles. Calm, I was very calm, with ice water in my veins. I remembered everything about him, his breath, his skin, every bit of it, the woman next to me drunk and going on about some bullshit, rubbing her hand up and down my thigh.

I remember reading somewhere how the Apaches used to tie soaked cactus needles around their prisoners and as the cactus needles dried up in the sun they slowly pushed into the prisoners' skin. I regretted my lack of imagination, and why I didn't pay better attention to those old Holocaust films they used to show in high school. Maybe I'd carry him around in the trunk of my car all the way to K.C., looking for the perfect place to light him up for good.

I told Shauna or Sheena or whatever her name was to meet me at this motel I knew of in a couple of hours. Told her I had some real important business I had to take care of. She pouted about it for a little while, then stuck her tongue in my ear. But all my attention was on Loverboy. He sat there staring at nothing, his jet-black hair slicked back like a Mexican. You'd never think to look at him what he done to me. He was about five-seven, maybe 160 pounds. I'm six-three and 220, so I didn't worry about taking him. Wouldn't have mattered anyway.

Two hours is a long time, baby, she hissed in my ear, but it was like a fly buzzing around my head. She'd be there or she wouldn't be, and I didn't give a fuck one way or the other. I figured she'd find somebody else as soon as she left the table. But she got up and left me alone, rejoined her other drunk friends out to get laid. Then it was just the two of us, him sitting there and me studying him all over.

'Member me?

I'd say. Then we'd slowly get reacquainted, dear old friends who went way back and belonged to the same country club, sipping julep, no grass stains on our tasseled loafers, not a single hair out of place.

Fred, I'd say, or Clifford, or Connor, why don't we step outside for a moment: I have a private matter I'd like to discuss with you—

You dream about payback, don't tell me you don't, about the ones who do things to you and what you'd like to do to them: you make up scenarios in your mind and work it out step by step, stalking your prey, cutting off any chance of escape. I didn't even know his fucking name.

An hour later he pays for his drink and walks out the door. I follow him. A few cars and trucks in the parking lot, he's walking and staggering just a little to this piece of shit Impala. Nobody's around, stars out twinkling like polished doorknobs.

Hey, Dick, I saw you in the bar, I said—

And the priceless look in his eyes, surprised and confused and Who the fuck are you?

My name ain't Dick, asshole, he says.

I saw that you were drinking and staggering a little bit there, Dick, and I wouldn't be a good citizen if I let you get in your car and drive, so why don't I take those keys off your hands?

He blinks once maybe, maybe twice, not understanding.

Your keys, Dick. I want your fucking keys.

More staring. More non-understanding. This is going to be better than I thought. I reach out with an open hand

128

like his daddy, his guardian, like I grounded him from play school.

Give me the fucking keys.

He wants to reach for something, but I'm too close.

Don't you remember me, Dick? The beautiful time we spent together in the LCC? The memories, the laughs? Me and you and your merry circle of friends?

I never seen terror open up in someone's eyes like that, his own 9-11 happening out under a single flickering streetlight with no one else around. He must have looked like that when he was a little kid and got caught whacking off in the bathroom for the first time, or watching some horror movie late at night, only bigger, so much bigger, with pieces of the sky falling down all around him and me towering there in front of him like the wrath of God.

He went down fast when I hit him, so fast I thought he'd fallen through the ground. I picked him up by his hair and smashed his face against the side of the car like his head was a cash register that just wouldn't shut. A tooth popped out of his head like a grasshopper. I knew I was getting a little carried away but I just couldn't help myself. Afterward I took off his belt and tied his hands, took off my belt and tied his feet. Stuffed a do-rag from the back seat in his mouth, put him in the trunk, then lit out on the road.

It was like the first time you ever got a blowjob by a woman who really knows how to do it, only better, baby, so much sweeter. I smoked his cigarettes, kept it at 70, and drove about forty miles like that.

But you know, it was already almost over even then. I

could feel it leaking out of me. I switched the radio to a classical station, something I'd never done before. Seemed more appropriate somehow for what was going down, those soft violins playing deep in the night. I kept trying to think of what he did to me to get in the right wrathful frame of mind, but for some reason I just couldn't do it. Everything happened so fast, like it was a dream or a TV show cutting from scene to scene, no way to keep up with it. The violins were having a strange effect on me after the adrenalin rush of pounding on his slicked-back head.

I was only carrying out what any man would do after what he did to me. He was like manna falling from the sky. Maybe I'd even let him smoke a last cigarette, something civilized because I wasn't a barbarian. I pulled over after a little while, but it wasn't to kill him. I got out and went to open the trunk, and then I saw it.

I saw it.

Without realizing it I had driven all the way out past Point Blank, like I was going to her house again, the same house I hadn't been to for years. A single light was on and that was strange because why would a blind lady need a light on in all that empty land?

I wanted to tell Dick about it, but I couldn't find the words. I opened the truck and there he was, bleeding and broken all to hell and needing medical attention bad. I was running out of time. Either I was gonna end it or I wasn't. I wondered if maybe she'd had it installed after we broke in, just to give the appearance, you know, of someone living there who could see. But that didn't make sense. She wouldn't do that.

Maybe it was just Miss Marian herself, glowing in the dark, generating just enough light so that people like me miles away could see it and say, Look: look at that light. I know the woman who lives there.

I closed the trunk on him again and got back into the car. But something was wrong, like I didn't know where I was going anymore. So I sat there in a daze.

Forgive? Forgive?

You fucking kidding me? After what he did to me?

That's too much to ask of anybody. So finish it, then. What are you waiting for?

Fuck forgiveness. Fuck mercy.

They never did a fucking thing for you anyway. So go on, take care of it, then get yourself that piece of ass with that sexy space between her two front teeth.

You got voices, don't you?

Voices that talk to you? That say things? Soft voices, clear voices, loud voices, bad voices, good voices? You hear them talking in your skull, *Listen to me: Do what you set out to do and don't hesitate over it. Take the motherfucker out. Finish what you started.* So I take him to this state park I know, park at the edge of this ravine, and then lift him out of the trunk. I lay down right next to his body and I hear him gurgling through blood. I'm laying next to him, dwarfing him, this pint-size rapist. We're laying there and I reach over and make sure he can breathe okay. Then I try out the words without even saying them, rolling them in my mouth like wet, gleaming stones.

I forgive you. I forgive what you done to me.

I know he can barely hear me. But I tell him about Miss Marian and I tell him about the fish. I speak it plain in language I know he can understand. I tell him about the minnows in the cage with the algae hanging off it and I tell him how clear the water was that day and how the fish appeared in the water with spots of shining glory on it, and Ms. Marian and everything else I think is important for him to see the picture of that day and the laughter of Mama's voice, like a bell ringing somewhere in heaven even then.

I take the rag out of his mouth then and another tooth comes with it. I wipe the blood away from his eyes. He's dazed, out of his mind, but he heard me: he heard what I said to him.

Please forgive me, he says, and starts crying. I don't know what makes me do it, but I take him in my arms and put his head against my chest. Maybe just living your own life is vengeance enough. Maybe it just is. Try to be good, Nathan, Mama said to me once. So here it is, Mama. I tried being good. The blind lady can back me up on it.

Gus

Munoz took off from the house seconds after the preach-er's dying speech, without a word to anybody. He just bolted and was gone, leaving the screen door swinging open behind him before it slapped shut with a pistol shot, the preacher's last word hanging in the air like the echo of a bell. He couldn't get out of there fast enough. The whole time the preacher was talking Munoz was staring razor blades at him and grinding his teeth, the chords of his neck sticking out like he was strapped into the electric chair. Munoz didn't believe a word of what the preacher said, and he was waiting to call him on it, though he never did.

Personally I don't think the preacher had any reason to lie to us on his deathbed, but that's just me. Others got their own way of looking at it. But it was clear that Munoz had it in for him and couldn't wait for him to die. You felt the resentment pouring out of his skin in invisible waves directed at the preacher's forehead. But it was strange and almost holy to listen to him go on like that, talking his blue streak, and even stranger to see the girl sitting at the foot of the bed with that peaceful smile on her face right up to the bitter end, Miss Marian beyond us sitting by herself in the corner, taking it all in with her blind eyes that looked like the scales of a dead fish glittering on the dock.

I've never watched someone die like that before and so we stayed till his soul was air lifted off the altar of the world. For a good night and a half it had been awkward and claustrophobic in the room, bordering on cabin fever, with the rain beating down as hard as five-penny nails, all of us shifting back and forth on our heels, wanting to get away ASAP but knowing deep down that we were watching something we'd never see again. We had to stand in the same rooms we had spray-painted and tore up with Miss Marian sitting there just staring at us without seeing anything, listening to every boot scrape, knowing exactly who we were, the perpetrators behind one of the worst nights of her life.

Having this dark guilty knowledge does something to you, rolling back the years to a single night in time you dearly wish you could relive all over again. I'll always know I could have said or done something before they got carried away, but to my everlasting shame I just sat there, stoned out of my mind with drool dripping off my chin. I didn't do a damn thing, just watched my so-called best friends go on a rampage that should have brought screaming eagles down on our heads, knowing even in my fucked-up delirium it was the worst thing you could do to someone, specially a blind lady like Miss Marian who lived by herself out in the country.

And that's been the hardest thing: knowing what we'd done to her and having to stand there while the preacher raved his head off down winding roads of remembrance. I think that's what got to Munoz, how we had to stand and listen to some guy we'd never met before ramble on about things that didn't make any sense. Watching someone die wasn't a big deal to him: he'd seen it all before. But there's no way to get him to talk about Iraq, though you can tell it's eating him up big time inside.

We used to talk about how we'd get out of Point Blank the first chance we got and never look back, but the truth was we always ended up crawling back here somehow. The list of our setbacks was almost too much to bear: Oly living out in an old abandoned dugout off Highway 5 after Cindy threw him out for good, Yarborough out of prison from doing time again for stealing, me holding down a series of dead-end jobs while I looked after Miss Marian and Aunt Tish (who's almost ninety years old), and Munoz coming back from Iraq so quiet it was like he's not even the same guy anymore, the one who used to brag about how all he wanted to do was try out his lethal skills in a country far away.

I always believed you could trace it back to what we did to Miss Marian and her house that night but I've never said it to anyone. Somehow things have a way of coming back to haunt you and there's nothing you can do about it. In my heart of hearts I wouldn't change a thing about how much we've each struggled because of what we did—we deserve what's happened to us, the worse the better. I figure I'll go the rest of my life trying to make up for that night, doing whatever I can for Miss Marian though she's never asked me for anything, not a single, solitary thing.

We have this strange unspoken agreement between us that's probably something I cooked up in my mind, that I'll do whatever I can for her and she'll treat me like nothing ever happened, like I'm just this generous neighbor who goes out of his way to help her because he's got a good heart. But that doesn't tell the whole story, not by a long shot. I keep going over it in my mind from every conceivable angle and to this day I can't figure out why she didn't tell anyone about what we did. Truth is, I'm waiting and trembling for the day when she'll bring it up and tell me how much it hurt her, and then I'll get down on my knees and beg for her forgiveness. I'll spill my guts and howl like a dog.

Long as I live I won't be able to get rid of the picture of Yarborough throwing her over his shoulder like a small sack of potatoes before he took her into the back room to do what he did to her, which is another thing nobody's ever asked about because we're afraid to hear the answer. The hard fact is life has fucked us up good and proper ever since, in mysterious ways that none of us can get a bead on, the reasons beyond our power to grasp or put into words. And maybe this would have happened even if we'd been choir boys, seeing as we all come from Point Blank, which everyone agrees is at the edge of nowhere with nothing to do except get high or get into domestic disputes, which is exactly how Oly got thrown out on his ass in the first place. I don't know. Just no way to figure it. We used to fancy ourselves some pretty badass dudes and maybe we were once, but when you get right down to it we're made of flesh and tears and heartache just like everybody else.

I think of Oly out in his dugout, making up plays for the Huskers in the dirt, all xs and os and blackboard schemes with half-time speeches he's rehearsed a hundred times. He's written them down and laminated them on old Cracker Barrel menus, sticking them in the front of his waist like he's pacing the sidelines. He'll whip them out and start calling them as long as somebody's there to listen and probably even when there's not. He's still holding out for a coaching job at the junior high school, but with his track record there's just no fucking way. He used to be a different person once, the youngest of us all by a good four years and up for anything, as good-natured as they come and always willing to play the clown. Maybe it was all the drugs he did and that other demented shit, lighting his hands on fire once, just to get a rise out of us. He's stuck back in the glory days that weren't even his to begin with, Johnny Rogers and Turner Gill and Mike Rozier, rehashing fourth-and-one down in Miami when Osborne went for the win even though everybody knows he should have settled for the tie.

I go out to visit him sometimes to make sure he hasn't frozen his ass off or some other dumbass thing, and each time I come away a little more disturbed. It's like his mind is breaking up into eggshell pieces made up of blocking schemes. He's got himself a banged-up projector and a generator from Home Depot and you can find him breaking down game film on a makeshift tarp he's strung up on the dugout wall any night of the week. He sits there rewinding plays and talking strategy with a 12-pack close at hand and a stack of porno magazines he calls the pussy posse next to a piss-stained pillow. Right before you get to the dugout you can see this weird light strobing out of it like one of those old-time Frankenstein movies where Frank starts walking toward you and reaching out, wanting to crush you in his arms.

I never thought one of my best friends would end up living in a dugout with weeds sprouting up along the first base line, addicted to everything you can think of and sleeping it off each night next to towering stacks of bug-eyed hardcore porn. It makes me embarrassed for him and ashamed, like there was something I should have done for him along the way that I missed or forgot, or didn't think was important at the time. The bottom line is, we should have known better, considering that he's the youngest and his mother left him when he was five years old to grow up with an uncle who used to beat the living shit of him so bad that once he even hit him with a waffle iron. I think we exposed him to shit he's never recovered from, like the time we snuck into Corey Snider's hayloft and watched him have sex with that sheep. We were sitting up there trying not to make a sound or laugh out loud but you could tell by the look on Oly's face afterward that he didn't think it was funny, not by a long shot. And it wasn't funny, just the most twisted thing you could imagine, Snider's bald head bobbing up and down with that sheep under him, gagged and tied up with a do-rag.

Later Oly told me with tears in his eyes that he couldn't get the picture of Snider out of his head, or how the poor sheep kept trying to kick her legs out. He said, *We should have done something for her, Gus—we should have put an end to it. I'll never wear a sweater ever fucking again.* But, like so many other things from those days, I didn't know what to say, how to respond to the bad things I saw going on around me. It's like I was frozen inside. I couldn't tell him that Snider used to break down crying in M's Diner, that he went to the Baptist church every Sunday and grew tulips and daffodils. I couldn't tell him that because for some reason it was so much easier to think he was just some perverted animal lover.

Munoz and Yarborough I don't know about because they've been away to prison or the war for so long—and these have made them go deeper into themselves, like ingrown toenails, suspicious of everyone they meet and keeping the people they talk to in front of them where they can see their every move. I've noticed that about both of them since they've come back. I forget whose idea it even was to go fishing at the tank again after all this time, but it had been at least a good ten years since the four of us were together, like we were suddenly drawn back to the place we used to know by some strange kind of undertow pulling at us without our knowledge or consent, all of it swirling down a drainage ditch somewhere under the big empty sky of western Nebraska. The fact is, I think we're lost somehow, licking our wounds in private and confused at what has happened to us and afraid about where we might end up.

I figure if I can just keep looking out for Miss Marian and

taking care of Aunt Tish then that'll keep me focused on what I need to do, out of trouble and away from my own fears coming down like hailstorms on the horizon. I've thought about getting my GED and going to school to become a nurse, but who ever heard of a country boy becoming a nurse, especially with my whole body covered with skull-smoking tattoos and signs of the Apocalypse? I don't even know how to ask about it without people thinking I'm a queer. For years I've wanted to tell Miss Marian that I'm different now, a changed man, not the same wild-assed punk who helped break into her house, that I'd do anything to take back what we did. But saying it so long after the fact can't mean a whole lot and I've come to realize that, too. I figure I gotta prove it to her through my actions and perseverance over the long haul, demonstrate it by the simple fact of being here for her.

Maybe I'm fooling myself—maybe I haven't changed a bit, just more aware of the magnitude of what we did and how it keeps spiraling out into outer space, only to end up back here warped into something huge that none of us want to deal with. I don't know. I don't seem to fucking know much of anything anymore. As the preacher was spouting off from his deathbed I kept watching Yarborough eyeing Miss Marian above the dying man's ravings, him looking at her as if there was a secret pact between them. Back then she was around fifty or so but still pretty good-looking for a blind lady, or any other kind of lady for that matter. Yarborough used to say things about her sometimes, things that were way out of line. But we let it slide: we made a fucking career of letting things slide. We never thought he'd actually follow through with it. But with the preacher dying in front of us there was no way to read his mind, no way to know what Y was thinking after all these years, if the night they spent in that other room was a memory he kept playing over in his head. I guess going to prison will give you that ability, make you poker-faced no matter what the situation.

I never much liked Y anyway, even though we grew up together. He always had a mean streak that made me uneasy, like he was always out to prove something. At the same time I couldn't help admiring him, like I was some kind of june bug attracted to a zapping porch light. It was hard seeing him watch Miss Marian like that after I'd come to know her on a daily basis, myself going through the radical transformation of being so afraid of what she had on us to organizing my whole waking life around making sure she was safe and taken care of, that no one would ever hurt her or take advantage of her again. I'd kill the sonofabitch who even so much as tried. Besides, it was pretty obvious that each one of us had failed and fucked up like any other loser in town, that we weren't so tough after all, that we had lost our way though we used to be so cock-sure about anything we put a hand to, at least on the outside. We'd had our chance like any other asshole and blew it sure enough, our lives dripping like rainwater through the sagging boards of a broken porch.

I guess when you're eighteen you think you can get away with anything and you'll never have to pay for it, though it has a funny way of coming back to kick your ass. I have no problem with that. I want to think it's a bad dream I keep having, that it happened in another life that wasn't mine.

Some nights I wake up sobbing like I'm choking back the moon, trying not to swallow all the bitterness and regret and the tides that feel like they're pulling me out into the middle of the ocean to drown me in waves of misery. I know that's part of the reason I look after her the way I do, patching her roof and mowing her lawn for free and running errands into town, getting her groceries and prescriptions and packs of Juicy Fruit, anything she wants or needs. I even got her a new set of false teeth because she mentioned once in an offhand way that her current set was causing her problems, so I went ahead and got her some. The last thing I want her to worry about is not being able to chew her own food.

I keep the teeth at home in the fridge, sitting in the cold dark for the time when she might need them. I take them out once in a while and put them on the table while I'm drinking a few beers, and I talk to those goddamned teeth like they're a second string quarterback who's waiting for a chance to get into the game. It's true they're a little creepy without a mouth or face to put them in, but they're grinning all the same, like tiny tombstones lined up in a row. I tell those teeth things that make me blush just to think of them, how I keep having this fantasy of forgiveness, where Miss Marian finally tells me that she's put it all behind her. And this is how it happens: I've been out working in her yard on a hot summer day and I come in for a glass of water. I'm standing next to the sink I installed for her, and Miss Marian hears me from the other room. She walks into the kitchen with quiet footsteps and says, *Danny, there's something I've been meaning to tell you for a long time. Why don't you sit down.*

GUS

I sit down with that glass of water, though it's shaking in my hand. I've been waiting so long for this moment that when it finally comes I can hardly keep my nerves from getting the best of me. She walks up behind me and puts her hand on my shoulder, and it's a cool hand, like a breeze that brushes my shoulder, and I close my eyes knowing she can't see the difference. For a second I want to be like her in her blindness and never see again; I don't want to see her face when she says, *It's about what happened that night.* Because then I'd lose it in front of her and ball like a baby, me a grown man over six-two weighing close to 260 and almost forty years of age with tattoos covering 90 percent of my skin, sobbing and weeping after an old lady, who can't see, has brought up the crime against her that I was a part of over twenty years ago.

I want her to say those magic words to me so I can somehow move on with my life that's been stuck in third gear ever since. I've come to love Miss Marian and maybe I always have, because she lived her quiet life the way she wanted without explaining it or apologizing to anyone, which is probably part of what set the whole thing into motion, people making comments about her in town behind her back, saying how she was kinda stuck up in her independence, living by herself without asking favors even though she was blind, nice to everyone she met but not afraid to speak her mind. People weren't used to that, didn't know what to make of her example. Then all the fancy clothes she made and wore herself making her almost look like a blind movie star, covered in a fancy white lace shawl that Yarborough said kept him up at night just thinking about what was underneath it.

Even when we broke in high as satellites and laughing like a pack of hyenas she didn't get hysterical or even so much as raise her voice, just stood her ground trembling with that shawl wrapped around her shoulders like a layer of fresh snow. I'll see her standing there 'til the day I die, like this little package of glowing seeds that could be jewels or just the water light dripping off of them. She was afraid but she tried not to show it, and you couldn't help but admire her for it even then.

Boys, she said. Just *Boys*.

And it wasn't like she was talking down to us, just *Boys*. I guess if it was any other word it could have even sounded like she was welcoming us somehow, like she was saying *Come in* or *God bless you*, which had the effect of setting off Yarborough more than anything else, the fact that she could just stand there and greet us in this calm and picture-perfect way. At that point I think we were all so surprised that we were ready to turn tail and leave because her reaction was the last one you'd ever expect. But Yarborough wouldn't have it.

I'm no boy, he said, *I'm a man. And I'm gonna prove it to you.*

But there's nothing to prove, Nate. Christ, can't you see that? Look at her: she's no bigger than my niece, who's not even twelve years old. She doesn't look down on us. She's just living her own quiet life out in the country. She doesn't have a gun, a dog, a phone, a pissed-off son or husband, a high-pitched scream or cuss word to throw at us. Not a goddamned thing. She doesn't even lock the fucking doors. Jesus, Nate, the woman can't *see* us. We can just walk away from her, no harm, no foul—no need to explain it to her or to ourselves, no need to apologize, no nothin'. We can just walk away.

That's what I would have said to him if I could go back and say it, what I keep trying to tell him even now when I think of it, trying to make him understand that there was no challenge here, no danger, that it would be like pushing over a gumball machine: there's no daring in it, not like any of the other death-defying shit we'd pulled off before to add to our growing legend, like playing chicken at 105 on local access roads, blowing up barns, free-basing name brand chemicals, branding each other with pliers to see who'd pass out first. We didn't have anything to prove, we'd kicked ass everywhere within a hundred miles and people were afraid of us. We didn't have to do this thing, whatever it was gonna be.

But Y never would have listened to me anyway. I know that now. He didn't want to hear it. He didn't want to hear her even say *Boys* or any other word. He had made up his mind that we were gonna go out there and follow through with what we had talked about no matter what, whether she begged for her life or said we could do anything we wanted. It wouldn't have mattered. The way he figured it we were bad-asses of the first degree and we weren't gonna bow down to nobody, certainly not a little blind lady living by herself.

There's a mystery to darkness just like there's a mystery to light, and we are both of them at the same time and no one can come to the end of it and explain what it means. Now whenever I'm at Miss Marian's house and it's sunny out I make up some excuse to go down into her basement. I tell her I'm going down to check on the water heater or some other such thing, but really it's something else I have in mind, this strange ritual I've grown into like a horn. I can't even say how or when it began, like it's been waiting for me my whole life to claim it.

I go down there and knock around for awhile, making some noise so she thinks I'm doing what I said I was going to do, but after a few minutes I sit down in a halo of sunlight pouring in from the cellar windows on the cold cement floor. I sit down Indian-style among these empty mason jars I've lined up in a row so they almost look like a happy smile, and I watch the jars brimming so full of sunlight they almost blind me, twenty or thirty of them, telling myself in a real quiet voice that I knew this light once in a deep-down way, knew it like a person almost, and someday I'll know it again.

There's laughter in the dust motes and something else besides, something so soft and gentle I feel like it's saying my name, saying it over and over again, out of the range of hearing.

Did I know this light in another life? Did it give birth to me in my mama's cry? I hear Miss Marian's footsteps up above, like rain falling late at night as you lay there wondering about the events of your life that rippled through you, leaving you behind. For some reason I can't figure out why it's important to sit in the basement of Miss Marian's house—the house I helped almost destroy once—in that halo of sunlight with those jars shining up at me for all they're worth. I'm not a pagan, but I think it's important for me to be there, to sup up that light with my whole body and try not to feel bad about what I've done and should have done.

Her blindness is like this other kind of light none of us can see, a rich, velvet blindness with smoke for eyes and the smell of sweetgrass drifting in the air. She lives in this dark mellow place all the time, and it must be like water at the bottom of a well or some other pure still thing waiting to break into rainbows. Her blindness only looks like a handicap from the outside, but it's what made her into who and what she is and maybe even why she didn't freak out like most people would have when we were standing there drunk and stoned in her doorway. Now I want to end up blind and quiet like her, I want to wake up knowing that everywhere I turn it's night, but night with the promise of a dripping star in it.

I sit in that basement and I wonder sometimes,

Who is Danny Gustafson?

What have I become?

Do my tattoos tell the story of who I am, or do they disguise the real person?

I got drunk for most of them, which is a given. I wanted to have the imprint of my rage stamped across my skin like the pimped-up graffiti you see on passing trains hauling chemical waste, something to show the end of the world or the Book of Revelation. I wanted to look like a crack house or a burning building coming down after a bombing, red, white, and blue ink flaring up out of the pores of my skin in blazes of glory with outstretched talons swooping down for the kill.

Then the day came when I ran out of skin except for my face, tattoos creeping up my body like mercury rising in a thermometer—and before I knew it I stood on some kind of threshold: my tattoo days were almost over. I could have cried because there was no skin left to conquer, just like some old famous general, and it was hard to breathe up there with all those violent pictures covering me, like my head stood on top of a landfill, white and pure as a baby's ass. I thought of ways of having my eyelids tattooed, the petals of my skin up there like delicate flower petals that never need to be watered, soft enough to poke a hole through with a toothpick. I thought about tattooing my earlobes, the inside of my mouth, the sides of my nose with Egyptian hieroglyphics, going all the way until I was a walking human kaleidoscope, the colors all swirling down the drain of the cosmos in psychedelic whirls with hula hoops spinning out of control.

But fuck that shit, too. You run out of skin and it's like you run out of life, the days dripping slowly by till there's hardly any left. It had to be special and I had to come to it in a radical new way, like a last will and testament, shouting to the world the struggle and triumphs of a lifetime going up in flames.

Then a vision came to me in a dream.

I saw my unmarked head, like I was floating above it, and I saw these deep blue lines with little stick people between them running for their lives in circles raying out from my eyes. I saw my face like a sounding map of the world's deepest oceans, places nobody has ever been with the stick figures teeming between them like crazed ants with pieces of fried hair in their mouths. Each stick figure was like something you'd see on an ancient cave wall, the story of the human race scrambling to get out of the way before the next major can of whup-ass explodes in its face, and I'd be the one to show them the history of the world, bigger and brighter than the bible or stories of the ice age with the baddest, brightest ink money could buy.

I want you to use something special for this last one,

I told the tattoo artist, who was like a father to me, the reader of my soul.

Use your best ink and make sure it goes down as deep as you can make it. Don't spare me any pain and draw it out if you have to. I don't wanna ever look at my face again without seeing those lines with the people running between them like miners scrambling for their lives. You gotta get it right because this is the last chance, the last unmarked skin I got to give you.

I begged, I pleaded with him, even taunted him that he wasn't good enough to even pull it off. But that was in the dream, the vision I had of the last tattoo. When I woke up it was all over: I knew I wouldn't go through with it, that my face would remain the way it is without any ink to darken it, even though this would strand me in limbo land where what was done was done and there was nothing more to do. For awhile I grieved at the thought that the last tattoo was over with, so I went out on a string of nights, picking fights wherever I could, just so I could feel my hard fist slamming into somebody or his slamming into me.

I couldn't use my body as an escape hatch anymore no matter how I tried. It would always be there mocking me for my efforts to turn it into a scrawl of blinding fury. It's strange to admit it now, but that's how it was. I wanted to wipe the slate clean and start all over, painting new pictures and carrying them around for everyone to see. But it was too late. I'd been cheated out of the colors I was sure told a towering truth, though when I look back on it now I can plainly see how bad they fucked me over.

Who was I outside of the tattoos and all the things I'd done to prove something to myself, to go down into all kinds of bad things in order somehow to be free? Even now, ass-naked in front of a mirror, I look like one of those primitive jungle people with plates stitched into their mouths who've never seen a wristwatch, my whole body covered neck to toes with blue and red ink coming up in a serpent's scales. I have a naked woman on all fours on both forearms and I used to be able to make them writhe in my own private lap dance. I should have joined the circus when I had a chance, where you can make your living as a professional freak in the gasps of thousands.

Why'd you want to plant a bad seed in me, man?

That's what I plan on asking Yarborough one of these days when it's just the two of us. We've been at cross-purposes all along and I realize it now. I don't have any bad blood left in me but I know what's right and what I have to do to try to make up for what we did. I don't know when Miss Marian became the focal point of my life but suddenly there she was, shining like a candle in the window.

You can't go back and change what you did, but you can sit awhile and pay attention to the light when it comes, listening to the blind lady's footsteps like they're tapping out some mysterious code. Then before it's too late you pick

up your mangled picture book of a body and get back to
the slow job of setting things right, weeding the flowerbed,
going to the store, working hard and honest in a hundred
small ways to let her know how sorry you are for what you
did, how you wish you could take back what happened, as
the light in the basement moves across the floor, taking the
guilt of a lifetime with it before the sun goes down into the
dark blooming sky.

Yarborough

So where does that leave us, preacher? What we gonna do now besides carry your ass out and bury it in a place where not even the coyotes can find it?

Dearly beloved, we are gathered here to bury the preacher before he goes bad. We are gathered here today because we came back to the scene of the crime from that night long ago, breaking into the blind lady's house as the preacher called us Lamb Bright Saviors and Munoz took off on his voodoo errand he wouldn't tell nobody about, and Oly's laughing, sobbing his crazy ass off even now, with Gus staring dewy-eyed at the blind lady as she sits there like the Rock of Gibraltar, and now we gotta find a place to bury him so we can try to figure out what he was trying to tell us.

So we gather.

And now gathered, we don't know what the hell it means or why, preacher shooting off fireworks in rapid-fire delivery

*while it rained ten hours straight, all of us closed up in the
blind lady's house like Old Mother Hubbard's. We are gathered
here today, though we're mostly just pissed off and confused,
standing and sitting here while my ankle monitor tells probie
where I am 24/7. We are gathered here and I don't know what
I'm supposed to do now that a stranger has died in front of us,
begging us not to call a doctor to save his life, so we didn't, we
let him die like he wanted, like it was early morning Christmas
with presents under the tree.*

And for what?

*Now we have to get his feverish ass out of here, carrying him
like we dragged the son-of-a-bitch in and dig a hole to bury him
in some out-of-the-way place way before he starts attracting
flies and FBI posters hanging up in the post office to announce
another missing person. We're supposed to be happy about this
and bursting with pride because he picked us: we're supposed to
think Halleluiah! He's shown us the light and we can finally do
what we were meant to do and get on with it, when I thought
all along I was perfecting the art of being an ex-con.*

Bet your sweet ass we gather.

*If you came all this way to die—if you meant for us to watch
you go and listen and pay attention to all the shit you spout-
ed—then what does it mean now, man? I mean, what the fuck
we supposed to do? Doesn't change a goddamned thing. We're
not any different for watching you die, except a little more on
edge for standing here hung over so long. So you knew about
what we did all the way down to some of the nitty-gritty details,
blowing the dust off old ghost chains and rattling them to get
our attention. Just smoke and mirrors, man, lady in the box
with a saw in your hand.*

What are we supposed to do with it, man?

What has changed after all your ranting and gnashing of teeth?

I still got a rap sheet with a felony on it.

I can't even get a job mopping the floor at Mickey D's.

Think we need you to tell us where we been and what we done?

Why doesn't Jesus take my life, preacher, instead of me giving it to him?

Why do I have to stand here and take shit from a dead peckerwood like you, in rhyming echoes that make no sense?

If you wanna talk to people on your deathbed then why don't you say something they can understand, instead of all your bullshit?

Just come right out and say what you gotta say.

Just say it.

I don't want to hear about light and lambs and all that shit.

I never asked for forgiveness.

It ain't yours to give.

I did what I did and I did it and I ain't sorry for it and nothing's gonna change that.

I pleaded guilty and I did my time across the board.

You can take your forgiveness and stick it up your dead stinking ass.

I don't intend on being no lamb.

I'm a lion.

I'm a killer in the sun, just like The Boss sings about.

And you ask, was it worth it?

Was it worth it?

The fuck you said that. The fuck you did.

You don't know who you're talking to, motherfucker.

I'll convince you, I'll show you how it is.

I'll. I'll.

I.

Why'd you say it, man?

Why'd you say those things? Why didn't you find somebody else to do your dying for? Who sent you? What does it mean? I wanna know. What you said. You can't just. All this time. All this fucking time. The waste like you said. Can't be true. Can it? Fuck, yeah, it's true. I'm not. No way. I can't. It just. Fuck. Christ. I don't. It's not that way. Can't be. I never was. Never not been. Preacher. Fucking shitting me. All the way out here. A lamb. No way. I got things to do, fields to burn. I ain't cut out for any of that shit. But you. You. I don't know what that is. What you said. Telling us all that. I ain't never been. Touched like you said. Did you mean what you said? I tried, I tried. A real man. A good man. A bad man. A man, just a fucking man, man. Never been able to touch it. Never been able to hold it. Thought I heard or saw it once or twice. Maybe. I don't know. What you said and described. The beauty of things. How it is. Never been there. Never knew. Nothing's like you said, man. But it's just like you said. It's true. It's fucking true. I've wasted my life. But I'm still here. I'm still alive. I still want all this shit I can't never have. Women, places, brothers, babies, tits, laughs, horse shoes, to be left the fuck alone. Nowhere I can't go to feel better about the shit, man. There is no fucking nowhere. Nothing's ever enough. But it's still too fucking much. That's all I know.

Everything's about to go up in smoke, I see it miles away and it's my life. But it's like there's nothing I can do about it. I can't afford to cry. You shittin' me? Crying? I don't wanna cry and I'm crying. I want a different throat to choke back on them. I want to fucking cry and stop crying and never cry again. Fuck those tears. I don't wanna live no more. I don't wanna die. I'm trapped in the middle and there's nowhere to go. People, they all have faces but they're full of crime. I've seen 'em. Deceitful as shit. They lie all the time and sometimes they don't even know they're lying—to their kids, to their wives, their men, themselves. Fuck the human race. But then it's morning and you gotta get moving, though you ain't even been to bed yet. And the world's around you so close, so close, with bad dudes breathing down your neck. You grew up and you became a man. You fucking lived, man, you lived. You didn't know what was right or wrong but just where life was and sometimes you went overboard and sometimes it cost you, man, it cost you a world of hurt on this planet of pain in a place nobody would ever visit you and everyone forgot you, like you never lived. You alive but there ain't nobody to know it. And there was nothing you could do about it—couldn't even hardly get pissed off because there was nothing you could do with the anger. Shit, preacher, you said what I mean. How you doing? somebody asks, and you can't answer and you keep on rolling, perfecting your tough-ass walk, and it's all catching up with you, so much dirt and you a big part of it and there ain't nothing to love, but that's all you hear is love, love, love, loving this and loving that, and it is so far away you can't feel you can ever touch it or be a part of it, but you gotta be, man, you gotta be.

Lamb bright savior, me, Nate Yarborough.

And you came all this way to tell us about it, to let us know. In a world that barks out noise and chemical clouds rising up on the horizon like charging horses. After 9-11, after Munoz come back with black holes for eyes staring off into space. And Gus probably some faggot and Oly still thinking he's somehow, some way gonna be a coach someday, though he's addicted to model glue. Who could make this shit up? But a part of it's got to be true. If you came all the way out here and been practicing this for years, then a part of it must be true. So we are. What you told us. We are loved. Okay. We are broken. All right. We are your brothers, your sons, your brides to be. Fuck if it makes any sense. Okay, all right then. I'll believe you. I'll believe what you said was true. Because of how you said it. Because of how you died. Because something in me says yes and I don't know why. Yes, preacher. Yes. I'll do it. I don't know what I'm even gonna do, but I'll do it. I'll become the words that came out of your mouth and they'll live in me, just like you said. I'm still here and you're not, and so I'll take what you said to me and live it up because it's the last truth that matters, the one that will somehow take all of this and turn it into a light that won't ever go out.

Munoz

You're going home, Shindig.

No more stops along the way, no more piss breaks or shooting the shit about what we're gonna do when we finally get back if we do make it back to the good 'ol U.S. of A.

I still can't believe you're a fucking virgin, but I'm not gonna raz you about it anymore.

Those days are over.

'Cuz we're almost there, Shindig, maybe two, two-and-a-half hours out, just like I promised you, man.

I told you I wasn't gonna let you down.

You didn't think I was gonna renege, did ya?

No way, man, no way: we been through too much together to fuck around with that.

Can you see okay, man, sun not in your eyes?

You wanna be up on the dash?

I know you can't see but you know what I mean.

Nobody will see you up here, I promise. Not with this tinted glass.

I'm even playing country for you, Shindig, because I know you like it, though you know I hate this redneck shit. But I'm doing it for you, Shindig.

That preacher, man, you wouldn't believe it. I can't get him out of my head. Could hardly make out what the fuck he was saying half the time, but his voice stays with you, ya know? It almost sounded like he was gonna start singing sometimes, but he didn't. I had to get out of there right after he died, way too claustrophobic in there.

I mean, I seen plenty of people die—but I ain't never seen somebody go down like that. He was *getting into it* bro, like he'd been rehearsing it for years. We didn't even know what he was dying from, some fever or nerve disorder, but he wouldn't let us call a doctor, begged us to let him die like that and go on the way he did. Still don't know what the fuck to make of it.

Believe that, man?

He just went on and on and on and on—and sometimes I wanted him to die just so he would shut the fuck up and other times, other times I gotta admit I couldn't *not* help listen to what he was saying and try to decipher it: talking about fish and flowers and buffaloes, marrying him on his deathbed, crazy shit like that.

I look like a lamb to you?

What do you think, Corey?

Maybe there's a grain of truth in it somewhere, I don't know.

Maybe he really did come all the way out here to die in front of us like he said: nothing can hardly surprise me anymore, especially after what you went out and did.

You never know, Shin, never can tell.

We just found the dude two days before.

But I felt you pulling at me out there in the dark—and I had my brotherly instincts to take care of because you're like this pain in the ass I can't stop worrying about till I make good on the promise I made to you. I don't how the fuck you extracted that promise out of me in the first place, Shindig, you must have used voodoo and the Virgin Mary—I'm not in the habit of promising anyone that I'm gonna smuggle them back into the country in a duct-tapped jar of formaldehyde and drive them thirty hours to the edge of fucking Wyoming, man.

You gotta know that by now.

I mean, don't you? Don't you?

Thing about you, Shindig, is you say about as much being dead as you ever did when you were kicking, and that's pretty fucked up right there.

You gotta admit that's fucked up.

It's fucked up, man.

Because I'm just saying, Shindig.

I'm just saying.

Here we drive all this way and stop in Point Blank because Gus gets ahold of me and we find that preacher passed out on the road with the girl and the wagon stacked with bibles. What would Vegas give me on that action, man? A million, a billion to one? I told you about Y and Oly and Gus: I wish you could have met them. I was thinking about taking you to meet them, but I didn't want to freak their shit out. So I kept quiet about you, though I wanted to tell them about you and what you did back there and all the rest of it, but I couldn't bring myself to talk about you somehow.

I mean, I want to tell everybody, I wanna broadcast it to the nation. Someday I will, when I get some kind of objectivity. But I realized a couple hours into it that there was no fucking way I could explain it to them, not then.

But I don't want you to ever think it was because I was embarrassed or ashamed of you, man: don't you ever fucking think that.

You hear me?

Just because you died for us don't mean you can lord it over me from the Great Beyond—no fucking way that's gonna happen.

I'll take you out of Casper and deposit you someplace else, someplace I know you'd hate.

So don't make me do it, man.

They wanted to hear about the last tour, but I didn't know what to say, Corey: I just sat there and drank with them till I was wasted in a way I haven't been for years, because all that time not drinking in Iraq cleaned my liver out and it resisted going back to the hard-drinking days. I puked my guts out and didn't say a goddamned thing. I kept silent about you. I didn't want them to feel sorry for you, or get the wrong idea: anything but that. I don't think I could take some kind of misunderstanding at this stage of the game, know what I mean?

I just couldn't fucking stand it.

That's why I had to get out of there and take you home, like I promised. You're a hero and you saved our fucking ass. I'm gonna find a way to tell it so people can know, a part of American History 101 forever, PFC Corey Shindig, who went out unarmed to offer himself up for a platoon that didn't want nothing to do with him. It would be a great movie, man, running *Saving Private Ryan* right into the ground. It don't matter to me that they cut off your head and took away your body.

Don't matter to me, Shin, don't you see?

They didn't get the best part of you, man, they didn't get your heart, they didn't get your *soul*. That's what I'm trying to tell you. Don't ever doubt that. You don't have to feel bad or embarrassed about it, man, you don't have to be ashamed. You're a hero, and no one can ever take that away from you. You don't look pathetic or morbid or any of that shit to me. I don't give a fuck what anybody thinks. I know the fucking truth. And I'll tell Mary Beth about what happened, you don't have to worry.

So don't sweat a thing, man.

I was wrong about you, Shin, as wrong as a body can be. But you gotta admit you weren't the most promising marine the Corps ever saw when you first came in. You weren't exactly lighting the world on fire. I always thought you were lost in your own little world, too much in your own mind, man, whacking off to that picture of your girlfriend, which you're not ever gonna live down even if you're dead.

But shit, listen to me: listen to my critiquing when you went and did what you did.

You're the only one who had the balls to do what nobody else would do, and here we thought you were the weak link in the chain.

But fuck us, man: fuck us. We were wrong.

That don't mean I should make a throne for you or nothing. Just so we got that shit straight between us, man.

Understood?

You know, Shindig, you don't look so bad. Really, man, I mean it. I seen worse. If I could I'd give you my arms and my legs and my whole body, man, because you gotta admit you weren't the most *imposing* motherfucker out there. I'd give them to you in a heartbeat. Now my dick, man, that's another story: we might have to negotiate on that, some kind of loan or something. You never used yours as far as I could tell except to shake hands with and mine's a heat-seeking python. I'm not sure you could handle that kind of manpower, Shindig. You might faint like a schoolgirl, man. Might light your shit up. That wouldn't do, Shindig, wouldn't do at all. But knowing you, you still wouldn't use it, would you?

You'd politely *refuse.*

No thank you, Munoz, I have my own little pee shooter right here: I'm quite happy with it, thank you very much.

Fucking Shindig, man: quietest little man-eating fucker around.

But I been wondering about something, Shin, wondering ever since it happened. You know, man, that day. How it went down. You out there alone under the white-hot sky, walking out, us back at the Humvee, I can still see your shadow out there, the outlines of it, the way it carried your body in a way I didn't know a shadow could.

I was wondering what was going through your head, Shin, you know, as you were walking out there all the way to the last moment.

Last night I dreamt I was you as the blade came down, and my last thought was how I always wanted to fuck Britney Spears and would never have the chance, man. Another night it was Marcia Brady from the Brady Bunch. And other times it's real profound, like, I've seen the face of God and he's a Muslim. I've seen the enemy up close and the enemy is us. Or just let it be, man, let it come down—the blade, the war, Bush's own fucking head, the sand, the minarets, the call to prayer like a wailing wall at the end of the world, all of this biblical crazy shit.

This is strange to say, Shin, but this is what I keep thinking, man: you looked peaceful to me, Shindig. As peaceful as someone can be when someone's about to cut off their fucking head.

Is that true, man?

Is that even close to the truth?

Or was it all just so surreal you didn't have a thought, which is understandable?

Is that how it was?

I thought you were looking at me, but I can't be sure now.

I wanna be sure about least that, man.

Were you looking at me, Shindig?

Were you sending me a signal of some kind?

Just wondering what you were thinking is enough to drive me fucking crazy.

I mean the first two days we're back in the states, you know what I go and do, man?

I go out to a gun store and buy some rifles and two semis and a hundred rounds, man, and I don't even know what the fuck for.

It's like I'm on autopilot and I just buy the shit up. I got some in the trunk right now, man.

Fucking believe that, man?

But I'd give all of it away and everything else I own if I just knew what you were thinking at the end, Shin, what was going through your mind.

Think sometime you could give me a hint?

Or am I way out of line here, man, strictly off-limits territory?

I understand if that's the case—I completely understand. It's just if I can't tell you about this, I can't tell nobody. Maybe you were thinking about Mary Beth, or praying, or asking for something, anything. Maybe you were saying good-bye to everything you ever knew. Maybe you weren't thinking anything, which probably would have been the best thing. Because it must have hurt like a motherfucker when the blade came down, but maybe you couldn't feel it, right? Tell me you couldn't feel it. Shock and disorientation, but you couldn't feel it, right? I know this is a fucked up thing to say, but you didn't *look* like you felt it. I mean, maybe I'm projecting to make myself feel better, but it didn't look to me from where I was that you were in a lot of pain. It didn't look that way to me.

You almost looked, you almost looked *relieved*, man.

Is that true?

Were you relieved that it was over, Shindig?

God, you have no fucking idea how I want that to be true. Two seconds after it happened we all wanted to be in your place, but that's pretty lame to say now, isn't it? Pretty fucking easy to say?

Don't answer that: I know it's fucking lame.

But I shot the motherfucker dead who did it, man.

I cut him down the same as he cut you down.

Almost anyway.

Here we got all this firepower and it couldn't match a sword, man. There's a lesson in that somewhere, man, but I don't fucking get it. I don't think I ever will. I ask about it, because, well, I don't know why I fucking ask. Because it's so clear in my own head, how you were kneeling there, how you went down, over and over.

I can't stop playing it over in my mind.

Like this preacher, man. I told you about the blind lady and what we did when we were punks. Still can't fucking believe it. It was hard for me to tell you about it, because I didn't want you to lose respect for me more than you already have. Breaking into her house like that, busting up her place, then Y taking her back to do what he did, which nobody knows about. I'm fucking ashamed of myself, Shindig, what we punk-assed did. Fuck man, it's like I'm in the confessional or some shit like that. I try to find a reason for why we did it but I can't find one, not the drugs, not the booze, not because we were bored. It's a fucking mystery to me, man, this dark inside, the dark of what we did.

I wish I could go back and say, No way, man, no way: I ain't gonna be a part of it.

But it's like so much else, you just get swept up into it and then you're in the middle of some shit and don't hardly even know how you got there.

I know it's a cop-out, a weak-assed excuse.

There ain't no excuse, man. Not one.

But the preacher, man. The preacher.

Maybe you would have liked hearing him. I even thought like I was listening for you so you could hear what he was saying.

Maybe you would have understood him better than the rest of us, Shindig. I don't doubt it for a second. Maybe you would have been able to tell us what he meant, make it plain as day in your infinite wisdom.

I wouldn't put it past you, bro, not anymore.

You saw things better than the rest of us, you were always prepared to go all the way.

You're the only one who understands.

What am I gonna do when you're gone, man?

When I make good on the promise I made to you?

I don't know where to put it, how to process it all, man: there's no good place I can put it. I just see it happening over and over, and part of me wants it to stop and part of me wants it to keep playing in my head so I never forget, even for a second, what happened and what you did.

I got this special bullet—you know the one I mean, but then I gotta think about how you went out and it's like you keep pulling the rug out from under me, man.

Because you saved my life so I could live.

You won't even let me think about ending it, man.

You leave me no options but to keep on going.

I mean, it's not even a fucking level playing field.

I take you home and bury you, then what?

And here I am, asking advice from you, Shindig?

Bitching, crying, complaining to you?

It's like we suddenly swapped roles and you're sitting there saying, Who's your daddy now, Munoz?

Who's your daddy?

Course, you'd never fucking say that, would you, Shindig: you never even cussed, first fucking leatherneck I ever heard of that wouldn't fucking cuss.

So you got me by the balls every which way, don't you, Shindig—made me promise you something I never should have promised in the first place, went out and saved my life, and never cussed and never even had any pussy on top of all the rest.

That's what I call doing a fucking number on someone, like you'd been setting me up since day one.

Am I right, Shindig—you were setting me up the whole time with your choir boy/martyr/hero/haunting fucking ghost/virgin routine?

Well, it worked—it fucking worked big time.

Congratulations. You won.

I hope you're proud of yourself, asshole.

I hope you're satisfied, me driving you to Wyoming just like you knew I would.

Otherwise why in the fuck would I be talking to you right now?

Answer me that, motherfucker.

Maybe you should make a promise to me in return?

Maybe you should offer to pay for a hooker or a stripper or something like that?

What do you think, Shindig—a couple of lap dances, a couple of blow jobs?

Least you could do for me.

You'd probably blush and shit, call the hooker Ma'am and open the door for her.

Shit, Shindig.

It's like there's nothing I can do one way or the other.

You and the preacher would have gotten along bigtime; you could have cozied right up to him and listened to all his bullshit, become the best of friends. I can see the two of you together, ying and yang, like two sides of the same coin. His speeches would have been right up your alley, Shindig, God talking on his back or mother nature herself speaking from the edge of the grave. You would have ate that shit up, Shin. Then you and the preacher could have hit the road and gone on tour as a couple of fucking freaks, a dying and babbling preacher and a headless war hero, taking the country by storm.

I can see it now, Shindig, your name up in lights—PFC Shin and the Deathbed Preacher blazing a trail of glory across America, getting on Larry King Live and shit, talking your rap, telling the rest of the country how it really is. You two could be famous, Shindig, loved the whole world over because you died for us and the preacher said the same fucking thing, dying so the rest of us could live. But how we're supposed to go ahead and do that I don't fucking know. You failed to mention that before you went out there, Shindig. And that's a big gaping hole you left behind.

I don't suppose you'd care to let me in on that little secret before we get to your hometown, Shindig?

Because we're getting closer, man. Won't be long now.

Then my obligation to you will almost be over, almost even, what I promised I'd do for you a long time ago in a different world and time almost, in a place where you seemed just about the only one who really knew what was going on and what it would take so the rest of us could see it, so the rest of us would know.

The ultimate sacrifice, man, the ultimate price.

This is it, Shindig, the last turn and the home-stretch to Casper.

We're running out of time. Our road trip's about over.

I can't hardly believe it, but I'm a little nervous, man.

Because then it really will be over, but it won't ever be over and I know that.

It'll be over but it won't be, one and the same.

But first thing's first. Get you to Mary Beth.

Tell Mary Beth.

Then we'll see about the rest.

Evensong

After the preacher spoke his furious last and died in a final sigh, the room dropped away to a forlorn emptiness and the buzzing of a fly that circled above his face to land on the beading purse of his upper lip, where it riveted a few times before taking off again for the wheat fields of his right forearm. The girl caved over his legs and started weeping, her sobs filling the quiet room like the quaking of a smaller but infinitely gentler earth. The one called O left again without a word, the others staring after him before returning their gaze to the dead preacher stretched out under his bedsheet shroud.

The girl's cries rose and fell in the room in peals of unbroken lament as the blind woman started to rock back and forth in her chair for the first time since the visitors had come into her house, the only sounds in the room for many minutes, until the girl pulled away and stopped crying, leaning back to wipe the tears from her eyes before getting off the bed. Then, with *sweet and painstaking reluctance and not so much as a spoken word for rationale, she started testing out a few dance moves on the wooden floor in her bare feet, doing a kind of primitive and sliding soft shoe none of them had ever seen: she moved slowly into the rhythm of the dance and they couldn't take their eyes off her, her sliding and scratching steps coming so soon in the wake of the preacher's last breath. She ranged and slid around the bed from side to side as the men all took an instinctive step backward to give her more space, her dance gathering in momentum and strangeness as she twisted and writhed around with her arms outstretched.*

In another time and place people had moved that way, had stepped and hopped and slid according to the dictates of an unfathomable tempo, to establish a harmony with all that is and the seasons of living and dying, the revolutions of the planets and the stars and the runoff from streams and rivers and human tears. She danced for each one of them, though they couldn't know it—could not understand the circumstances and the need that prompted her to move the way she did, sometimes seeming to drape herself across the floor in lascivious abandon and then to hop-to on one foot then another, like a schoolgirl skipping rope.

When she did her last pirouette and curled up in a ball on the floor they knew something momentous had occurred, though they couldn't say what it was. The preacher was staring up at the ceiling with a look of rapt amazement, his mouth slightly open like he was about to say something even then. When the girl got to her feet she looked different, not like the girl who had been hauling the wagon full of bibles but someone older and wiser. She smoothed out her dress and rearranged her hair like there was no one else in the room, sticking a barrette in her mouth to free both her hands as she slipped her long black hair into a ponytail. Somehow she had taken over where the preacher had left off, and they waited for her to say something. She looked like she was turning over a notion in her mind, then went up almost absent-mindedly and kissed the dead preacher's forehead.

She told them —

Mr. Gene's in your hands now, where he always wanted to be. So please be careful with him. You'll never know how much this meant to him. But maybe you might someday. As for me, I better get going.

She walked to the door, stopped, and looked back one last time.

Thank you for letting us come to your house, Miss Marian. I can see why they're in awe of you.

Then she left. Lacuna and aftermath of a barefooted girl's departure, twice anticipated by the departure of O. and the preacher's death. The one covered in tattoos looked at the others, clearing his throat to speak. But before he could say a word the blind lady said

You don't have to say anything, Danny. It's over. Take him and do what he asked. It's been a long day, but tomorrow we can start over after we all get some rest.

Mady

Now that Mr. Gene is dead and I danced for him like I promised, I'm going to walk all the way to Mexico, *todo la via.* Then I'm going to sit out in one of those cabanas they have down there, put my tired dogs up, and drink my first beer. After that I'm going to suck on a lime.

After that, I have no idea.

I never had much use for the future anyway. You can't poke at it with a Swiss army knife and nobody even knows if it's there to begin with, so I'm not gonna lose any sleep over it one way or the other. When the future becomes now then I'll pay it some mind, but then it won't be the future anymore, so why get all bent out of shape? Some might call it irresponsible, but they can officially go jump in a lake. I'm my own man now, I mean my own person.

Mr. Gene left me some cash and a canvas backpack he used to tote his notebooks in with all his writing. And I still have three packs of cigarettes, so what else does a body need? If anybody tries any funny business I'll vanish into thin air like the smoke above a magician's hat. America's a big country and I know how to get lost in it like the dirt on the back of somebody's elbow. I know how to hide behind the giant letters of a billboard and sleep under a bridge. If things get real bad I'll scrounge for food at the back alleys of restaurants. They're always good for a meal or two, sometimes for a whole week straight, depending on the cook's mood. I've sucked on pine needles before for vitamins. Sure, I can do it. I'm no stranger to making things work, whatever they happen to be. I've been surviving ever since Mr. Gene rescued me from the fire he had somebody set so we could walk across the country together. If any man wants to touch me he'd better be prepared for a rabies shot (not that I have rabies, but hell, they won't know that). I'm not above biting off a little finger and spitting it out for the whole world to see. But I hope to God it doesn't come to that.

It won't be the same without Mr. Gene, but I can't think about that now. If I think about him I'll just start crying again and that won't get me anywhere. I've got to stay focused, keep my game face on. So once they bury Mr. Gene I'm going to start walking south. I figure I can make it in about ten weeks if I don't get sidetracked or twist an ankle or get sicked-on by a dog. I'll just leave the wagon and the bibles. I was glad to pull it with Mr. Gene, but I'm announcing my retirement right here and now. No more leather headbands for me. If I never see another bible again as long as I live, that's okay by me. I know pretty much all of what's written inside of one anyway. The bible's all right if you got nothing else to read, but there sure is a lot of killing in there with salt sprinkled over everything. I was never tempted to eat it page by page like Mr. Gene did, but maybe I was missing something.

You never know.

I've heard in Mexico people aren't embarrassed to walk around in sandals, and that suits me right down to the ground. Shoes are overrated, if you ask me. I don't even want to hear about pumps. The only pump I want anything to do with is a bicycle pump or maybe an old-fashioned pump for a well in the ground. Otherwise I don't have any use for it. I'm itching to see if I'll fit in better down in Mexico if even half the stories I've heard are true. This one fella told Mr. Gene and me that he saw a dead horse on the side of the road with all four legs sticking up in the air, outside Cabo San Lucas, but everyone just went about their business like it was no big deal. This same fella said he went jogging through a whole city of garbage with dogs tied to cinder blocks snarling at him and black smoke coming up here and there like the whole world was burning to the ground. People lived right next to that garbage, but when they smiled their white teeth just about took your breath away. That's what this fella said anyway.

I want to see if any of that's true. Doesn't mean I'm gonna stay there forever. I've always just thought of it as a different kind of place where being broke isn't the worst thing that could happen to you. But maybe I'm way off. Mr. Gene used to call us a couple of rollin' misfits, and I see what he meant by it now: we could fit in about anywhere if we had a mind to, but then the road was always whispering our names and we got the urge to move again, and cleared out the first chance we got, no matter how many bibles we sold or who we ended up hanging out with.

I guess you could say it was just about the greatest freedom there is in the world, and I wouldn't change it for anything, just the two of us and the open road, going to places we'd never been with a stack of bibles in Junior Wobbly. We traded off hauling equal shares and I can't remember a single time we ever argued about it, so there was no need to complain. I would have made a great sled dog, only nobody would have needed to mush me. He'd pull for an hour using his headband, and I'd pull for an hour using mine. We had what you'd call a good working relationship, and Junior never suffered the worse for wear, I can tell you that. It had the best-greased wheels around and not a part of it rusted or squeaked.

We'd pull into a new town after midnight and old Junior was quieter than a canoe gliding through still water. You wouldn't even know we had us a means of conveyance and deliverance, as Mr. Gene liked to say. It's true sometimes I got a little tired pulling Junior around, but Mr. Gene never complained about it, so why should I? Hills were the worst if we couldn't bum a ride. They plumb wore us both out, and some days we wouldn't get even a third as far as we were shooting for. But you got to make a living somehow if you hope to eat and meet some folks, and if it ain't a wagon you can be damn sure it'll be something else you gotta haul around.

Most people we saw either A) ignored us and pretended we weren't there; B) tolerated us like we were retarded people that would wander off before long if they just patiently waited it out; C) really surprised and interested in what Mr. Gene had to say; or D) made fun of us and a whole lot worse. Course, the D's were the hardest — and long as I live I'll never understand why people get such a kick out of making fun of other people, I don't care who they are.

Like this time in an abandoned parking lot next to Wal*Mart in a small town in Missouri. Mr. Gene set up shop just outside of it and attracted maybe twelve people to hear him preach who were going to their cars. Mr. Gene was standing up on Junior for extra height, waving his arms around like a giant ice cream–colored bird. He had the goods when it came to getting folks' attention sure enough, at least for the first ten minutes or so. I was off to the side smoking another guilty cigarette when these folks came around in a little half-circle, out of curiosity. They were all ages, but I'd say most of them were older folks in their sixties. They probably hadn't seen anyone like him this side of a Barnum and Bailey circus. But then these three boys kind of wandered up and started poking fun at Mr. Gene on the sly, getting bolder and bolder. Before long they were laughing outright in his face, making nasty comments everyone could hear, and then the rest of the crowd went back to their cars and it was just those three boys jeering at Mr. Gene. At that point I was getting kinda nervous, so I lit another cigarette, but Mr. Gene was just getting started.

He had this strange ability to block out negative vibrations altogether, like he was riding the crest of a wave high above the rest of the people around him. Sometimes I think opposition even gave him an extra kick, like a booster shot in the arm. It was a hot day and Wal*Mart was busy, with people coming and going and revving out of the parking lot. Mr. Gene couldn't stand on the premises or we would have gotten busted for loitering and pandering. So it was some side-winding preaching he was doing, appealing to folks going by in neutral territory. The only ones who showed any staying power were those boys, who couldn't care less about what he was saying, just how he went about saying it. They were around twenty or thereabouts, two of them with seed caps on their heads and grimy faces, like they'd just come from working on their trucks. They had grease stains on their jeans and one had a goatee mustache that looked like a red triangle dripping off his chin with a blue flaming tattoo all up his left arm. By the way they stood there looking at Mr. Gene you would have thought he had come all that way just to be made fun of. It's true some of Mr. Gene's speeches went on a long time, but it wasn't like he was talking nonsense, just the only truth he knew. He wasn't a hell-fire and brimstone preacher anyway, more like a fancy dressed salesman that used all these made-up words because he didn't know how to say it for the truth burning up inside him.

Children, listen to me—there is no love like the love between strangers,

He told them, and it was hard to disagree if you really hunkered down and thought about it. All I'd ever really known were strangers, and I got so I could talk to just about anyone as long as they weren't out and out mean—didn't matter if they were black or white, young or old. I'd talk to a kangaroo if I knew the language. But those boys didn't want to hear what he was saying; they didn't want to hear about love or anything that would settle down in their souls. They thought the love he was talking about was a colorful t-shirt love you could put on and take off when you pleased, but it wasn't gonna pay the bills or get them better jobs. Least that's how I was reading them. I wanted to get in between Mr. Gene and those boys but they crowded in all the more. They wouldn't let him so much as finish a sentence.

What all can you do with this love? They asked.

Can you eat it? Can you sell it?

What if I pulled a gun on you, Mister, would you talk about love then?

And other questions like that, questions they didn't even want an answer to, just asking him to be mean back at them.

I'll give you a bible and you can find out for yourselves,

Mr. Gene told them, but they didn't want to hear that either. That's the kind of boys they were. One of them came right up to Mr. Gene and started playing with his tie, flipping it up and down. Mr. Gene tried to ignore it but the sweat around his mouth gave him away. I could tell he was getting a little scared, but he kept right on preaching. I think it went on for about ten minutes like that, every other word that Mr. Gene was saying being punctuated by that boy in his face, flipping his tie around.

Tell you what, preacher,

the boy finally said.

He said he wanted him to meet us at this out of the way place and then they'd spread the word and get him a good crowd, people who were ripe and ready for the word. The boy took a pen out of Mr. Gene's pocket and started writing down the address on a crinkled receipt he took out of his own pocket. Anybody could see it was a trap, but Mr. Gene said we'd be there. He didn't even bat an eye. Once he got an idea in his head there just was no talking him out of it. After the boys left I begged him not to go, to forget the whole thing so we could move on to the next town or place: I practically draped myself across his arm. But Mr. Gene wouldn't have none of it.

If I preach just to the people who want to hear it, what kind of preacher am I? And more importantly, what happens to that tiny part of the truth with which I've been entrusted?

So we went out to that deserted place, this abandoned warehouse on the edge of town. Even though it was hot out I felt a chill in my veins. Mr. Gene wouldn't even look at me. He was pulling Junior and had his head deep into the harness. All I could do was walk next to him and try not to sniffle too hard.

When we got to the warehouse there was shattered glass all over outside with weeds snaking up the rusty sides. You could tell it was no kind of place to meet somebody in. The front door was busted, with a spray-painted board nailed diagonal across it, like half of a railroad crossing sign. The windows were all shot out except here and there, like jagged teeth. I begged Mr. Gene not to go inside, but he just took off his headband and headed in without a word. The only thing I could do was follow him. It smelled something awful inside, like window cleaner mixed with overflowing toilets and these fifty-gallon drums all knocked over this way and that with trash and litter and broken bottles everywhere.

I didn't want to cry but I started to anyway real quietly, but Mr. Gene just adjusted his tie and looked around and began to hum a gospel tune. You know how you know when something bad is gonna happen and there's nothing you can do about it? But Mr. Gene could put out of his mind just about anything when it came to his preaching or deathbed practices: I never saw a more determined person in the face of danger or distraction. We waited there about twelve minutes, and then we heard them pull up outside in a sliding halt with country music blaring before they cut the engine.

What else can I tell you?

Here I've got off on a tangent about a story that can't be changed, wasting all this time and energy because you know how it's gonna end. You know it and I know it, and not even because I was there. They beat on Mr. Gene and held me down kicking and screaming in front of him but I couldn't get away: the boy who was holding me was too strong. Mr. Gene tried to speak once but they kicked him in the mouth, so he could only spit out blood and a few teeth like chipped dice.

Then when he was down for good, not moving, one of them took his hat and started to pee in it. Long as I live I'll never understand why he did that. Some people don't hardly even know what kind of meanness they're doing to someone, because if they really knew they'd never do it in the first place or feel so bad even thinking about it that they'd never be able to look people in the eye again. But of course that's not true, because this kind of meanness is still alive and most of the people who do it aren't ashamed of it one bit, like a dark miracle in reverse.

And there's no getting round that fact, if they knew what they were really doing. If they could take a step back and think about it for a second.

But see, in Mexico I hear they play these little guitars and you can get you one of those sombreros to keep the sun off. You can mish-mash the brim any old way you want so it fits you real good. And they have salt on the rim of a tall glass filled with tequila, and you can set yourself down there all day and sip on it, watching people walk by on the beach. You can buy flip-flops for a few pesos, wear 'em for awhile, then give them to somebody else who maybe needs them to patch up some rubber tires. Then one of those vendors will come up and try to sell you a watch or something, but if you get him into a conversation he'll tell you about his hometown and where he grew up. It won't be about buying or selling anything anymore but a real conversation between two people, *mano a mano*.

You'll notice his mustache and the stubble on his chin and he'll tell you his name is Juan. Juan will have this strange little habit of rubbing his belly and you'll think of a pot of boiling corn, where the kernels are staring sun-spots at you. And no one can ever say there isn't love in the most far-away places, in a cold bottle of beer with sweat beads dripping off it in a country you never been to, testing out your Spanish. *Hola, hombre. Como se dice beer, señor?* I know it'll be lonely sometimes, Juan or no Juan. Might even be dangerous and a lot different than I dream about. But I'm willing to take the chance. I always have been. The trick is to admit the danger and the loneliness is there and then open your palms to it on the sly. Say to all the dark, unknown things: Yeah, I see you. I know you're there. I can tell you're lonely too.

But even when you're lonely somebody's looking at you sure enough, even if you're in an igloo at the North Pole. I don't know how I know it, I just do. It could be a polar bear, one of those floppy seals, even a bunch of snowflakes falling slant-wise to the ground. And they're watching you, they're seeing what you do and what you don't do. They'll see you throw down your snow shovel or unzip your fly if you're a guy, or march around in little circles to keep your feet warm. The snow, the sea, the sun, the sky, your own shadow sees you and keeps watching, and even if you're by yourself you're not really by yourself, if you know what I mean.

I can't prove it exactly, but I don't lose any sleep over it. Seems as common as mud to me. There's nothing wrong in talking to a bird, a tree, or an ant running up your arm—nothing wrong at all. If there was, God wouldn't have given you a tongue to say their names. They're watching and they can hear you, even if they don't talk back. Even the blind lady sees you, just not with her eyes. Maybe by the palms of her hands or the grooves of her fingertips. That's what I'm gonna keep telling myself as I walk to Mexico to remind myself of the only truth that matters.

Somebody's always watching you, Mady Kim, somebody always sees you. And Mr. Gene ain't gone-gone, just gone. You can still talk to him if you want, only now his ears will be made of funny things, like Styrofoam cups and hub hub-caps on the side of the road. He'll see you walk all the way to Mexico, so when you finally get there and have yourself that first beer, you can put your feet up and raise that bottle high into the air and say, This is for you, Mr. Gene, then take that first sip and drink it down to the dregs, sunset and all.